Ashes of Faith

Ashes of Faith

A doomsday cult's orchestration of mass murder in Africa

Robert Bwire

Frontier Publishing

Ashes of Faith

ISBN 1-931882-70-3

Scripture citations in this book are taken from the Good News Bible: Today's English Version, which is readily and widely available in Uganda.

Photographs are courtesy of the *New Vision*, Kampala, Uganda.
Author's photograph: Annelore Bwire
Cover art: Gwendolyn Magee; photographic credit: Roland Freeman.

Frontier Publishing
Postbus 10681
1001 ER Amsterdam
tel: 020-3309151
fax: 020-3309150
fp@fsf.nl
http://www.frontierpublishing.nl

printed in China

To my beloved *Nguhwa* Riyaka for firing my imagination with mesmerizing tales of her semi-god ancestor Haderesa

Contents

Acknowledgments

Numerous people have contributed to the evolution of this book and to them I am deeply indebted. First I want to thank Teopister Agutu, an excellent Ugandan journalist, who worked tirelessly at every single stage of the manuscript. Teopister, I can hardly express my gratitude for your excellent in-depth expertise on the subject matter. Your constant encouragement sustained my interest in continuing researching the book. *Webale muno*!

I wish also to thank Charles Obbo for his generosity and support during the months that this book was being researched. Charles, I apologize once again for those annoying transcontinental telephone calls that seemed to only be possible in the middle of the night.

A very special note of gratitude is owed to the people who willingly volunteered information on the ***Movement for the Restoration of the Ten Commandments of God***. These included Roman Catholic priests, journalists, civic leaders and villagers in rural Uganda. Most of them are not comfortable to be cited by name—a sentiment that I feel obliged to honour. I can never thank them enough for their willingness to answer questions. I acknowledge this invaluable support by using the first person plural pronoun in much of the narrative.

Thanks to Lodovick, an old schoolmate, who first told me about Malachi and the ***Covenant Box***—I hope this book might help you and many others in the quest for the ultimate spiritual truth. Thanks to my friend Maria Geraldine who while growing up in western Uganda came to know Mr. Joseph Kibwetere as a respectable teacher and whose trust in the man has been irreparably damaged. Having lost an aunt at the hands of the wacky cult headed by Kibwetere, it must be particularly difficult for you and numerous other families that lost beloved ones. Maria, I mourn your calamity and greatly appreciate the discussions we held soon after the Kanungu fire. Thanks to the people at Frontier Publishing, and in particular to Filip Coppens, for their support, enthusiasm and firm endorsement. Heartfelt thanks to Gay Roberts for a fabulous and meticulous editing job. I also extend thanks to Jane Teasdale for reading the first draft.

And my heartfelt thanks to my children, Annelore and Tom, for all the joy; and my wife, Nelly, for kindness and continued support.

Chapter 1
In thrall of Christianity

False prophets appeared in the past among the people, and in the same way false teachers will appear among you. They will bring in destructive, untrue doctrines, and will deny the Master who redeemed them, and so they will bring upon themselves sudden destruction.
2 Peter 2:1

Of Uganda's estimated twenty million people, eighty percent are Christian and ten percent profess Islam. The rest of the population is said to belong to indigenous religions. Among the approximately sixteen million Christians, two-thirds are Roman Catholic, and the rest belong to various shades of Protestant denominations, of which members of the Church of Uganda (the Episcopal Church) form the majority. Quoting such statistics, however, is an oversimplification of the reality surrounding religious practices and beliefs in Uganda. For example, it makes the erroneous presumption that all who profess one particular Christian denomination have no room for other spiritual beliefs. Although some people may profess Christianity, a good proportion still find room for indigenous religious or spiritual practices, which involve ancestor worship; in some cases, it even includes human sacrifice. Interestingly, but not surprising, most of the successful emerging Christian groups are those that appeal to their followers by repackaging Christian doctrine with a touch of traditional flare. Bits of indigenous traditions sprinkled here and there are especially appealing to rural folk and poor urban dwellers.

When Ugandans get into religion they can be quite fanatical about it, as history testifies. Christianity was introduced into Uganda as recently as the late nineteenth century through the evangelising work of mostly French and Anglican missionaries. The first indigenous Christians were zealots when it came to observance of their new faith. So passionate was their belief in Christianity that they saw fit to defy the authority of the political institutions that had cemented their society from time immemorial. Their King was no longer the mortal who drew his right to rule them from a long dead ancestor, who had excelled in battle. The new King was an eternal God who dwelled in heaven where he presided over humans of all races and to whom he had shown great love by sending his only son, Jesus Christ, to die for their sins. It was an attitude that challenged the King's power.

As if the attitude of his subjects was not annoying enough, the King also felt that the missionaries were challenging his authority, which was a source of further irritation. For instance, once the missionaries had established a stronghold in the mighty, ancient Kingdom of Buganda they insisted on having a hand in the running of that nation. Their interference was not only limited to bigger issues such as Buganda's foreign relationships, but they were also keen to get involved in petty matters; they demanded, for example, a prominent role in the selection of young men to serve as pages in the King's court. So far, this had been the prerogative of the King and his closer inner circle of advisers. Pages entertained the King by singing songs praising his wisdom and valour or accompanied him on hunting trips. It was also from among the pages that chiefs and other administrators at local level were selected. The stage was thus set for a confrontation between the King of Buganda and the new Christian religion, which had succeeded in converting quite a sizeable number of the local population.

Among the converts to the new faith were men who belonged to the royal compound, where they served the King in numerous capacities. These included advisers, attendants at the royal court and even pages. Many of the boys and men in the King's compound were there to satiate his sexual desires. For King Mwanga, the powerful ruler of the mighty Kingdom of Buganda at that point in history, was strongly attracted to men[1]. Naturally he was incensed at the new religion that proclaimed that it was a sin for a man to have sex with another man. It was against this background of grievances that King Mwanga embarked on a deliberate, systematic and violent campaign to destroy the Christians in his Kingdom.

Among the first Christians whom he ordered to be killed was his favourite lover who had dared to challenge the King's lifestyle. It is recorded that in a maddening show of anger King Mwanga charged at the lad, driving the royal spear through the young man's chest. He then ordered that the young man should be beheaded and his lifeless body thrown into a huge fire. With this singularly macabre act, the campaign against Christians had begun in earnest. The next phase saw the King summoning his entire court. "Those who do not pray stand by me, those who do pray stand over there," Mwanga is reputed to have thundered in a most terrifying voice. In this way the Christians were separated from the rest of the group. To the King's chagrin fifteen men aged between thirteen and twenty-five years chose to identify themselves as Christian. Defying the King was an act of treason that was punished by death.

King Mwanga ordered that the Christian converts be bound and marched to Namugongo, a village some twelve kilometres east of Kampala, where dissidents were routinely beheaded. Among the Christians was a young man, Mbaga, whose father served the King faithfully in his capacity as chief executioner. The executioner beseeched his son to denounce Christianity, but Mbaga chose to identify himself with his brothers in the new faith. On reaching Namugongo the young Christians were wrapped in papyrus mats and burned to death. And whilst the fire reduced their bodies to ashes their joyous spirits sang hymns and chanted Christian prayers. Amidst the dancing tongues of flame and the crackling sound of burning cinders, the young men joyfully proclaimed, "You can burn our bodies, but you cannot harm our souls."

All over the Kingdom, converts to Christianity irrespective of denomination, were hunted and persecuted. A certain Andrew Kagwa, a county chief, had become Christian along with his wife. Mwanga ordered his execution too. Before being thrown into the fire, Kagwa is reputed to have delivered to the chief executioner the following courageous words that can only be mustered by those who are unwavering in their faith: "God will rescue me. But you will not see how he does it, because he will take my soul and leave you only my body." A total of twenty-six Christians were burned on the pyre on one single day—2nd June 1886. More Christians were killed at the orders of King Mwanga in the days and months that followed. The last official execution took place in January 1887 when a certain Jean-Marie Muzeeyi was beheaded. During those turbulent times a total of forty-five Christians were burnt publicly on the pyre for professing the new faith. In 1922 Pope Benedict XV lent a Vatican seal of approval to these forefathers of Christianity in Uganda by elevating the Catholics among them to a status of "Blessed". On 18th October 1964, Pope Paul VI canonised them.

Faith not only divided the traditional belief from Christianity; Christianity itself was divided. Relationships between the two mainstream Christian Churches, the Roman Catholics and Episcopal, have often been acrimonious. In the late nineteenth century, the two groups attacked each other repeatedly, all in the name of the God of love. Incensed Protestants torched Catholic churches and angry Catholics destroyed Protestant places of worship. It was a silly war considering that most of the believers did not fully appreciate the differences between the two religions except for the fact that the Protestant missionaries were mainly British and the Catholic evangelists originated for the greater part from France.

The two communities have been bitterly divided by these ancient sectarian rivalries up to this day; European divisions that have nothing to do with religion were thus transposed on Africa's soil. There is frequent squabbling over appointments to political office and in the public service. Disgruntled Catholics repeatedly level accusations at government for showing more sympathy and showering privileges to those of the Protestant persuasion[2]. When the then minister of education, a well-respected Protestant professor, closed down a number of Catholic-run colleges in 1999, citing poor quality of education as a reason, Catholic clergy and laity interpreted this as yet more evidence of a national Protestant conspiracy to stifle the progress of Catholics. So angry were the Catholics that for fear of becoming unpopular, the government reconsidered and reversed its decision. Pundits observing the Uganda political scene hailed the revocation. This was not an exaggeration especially if one considers the fact that most governments in Africa are not in the business of being impressed by public opinion.

Taking advantage of the right to worship enshrined in the constitution, many dynamic Ugandan entrepreneurs have formed their own churches. As a result there are over one hundred Christian religious groups scattered around the country. Most of the mushrooming Christian churches in the country are millenarian in nature, with a message stressing disquieting and terrible times awaiting the unrepentant world in the coming few years. Those who repent their sinful ways and follow the prophet (most of the founders of these groups refer to themselves as prophets), the groups claim, will be spared the terrible sufferings and tribulations. Some Ugandan church watchers note that a good number of the new religious movements are multimillion shilling businesses whose main concern is making money by shamelessly exploiting a poor and ignorant population.

The leadership of the new religious groups consist of men and women who claim to have received divine revelation. On a beautiful Sunday morning we decided to pay a visit to such a man at the helm of an outfit called the ***Covenant Box Descended into Uganda*** on the Kampala-Jinja highway.

Driving out of Kampala, Uganda's capital, we leave behind its seven hills, of which one boasts a monumental Catholic cathedral, another the colossal Episcopal Cathedral, and yet another hill is home to the massive Muslim mosque. On a fourth hill looms the beautiful Baha'i mother temple of Africa, the only one of its kind in sub-Saharan Africa. And as if to show how modern architecture and spiritual enlightenment can cohabit amicably in the heart of Africa another hill is home to the exquisitely built Abundant Life church where the "gospel of prosperity" is preached. The Abundant Life church is the place for Kampala's moneyed class. Here, shielded from the poverty-stricken multitudes in the slums of the city, the post-colonial plutocrats retreat safely for a moment of prayer. Finally, we get out of the chaotic traffic and head eastwards towards the relatively quiet town of Jinja.

We travel along a beautiful stretch of road that cuts through a cluster of small rural towns with colourful roadside markets offering an assortment of tropical fruits: yummy passion fruits, chubby pineapples, delicious sweet bananas, and mouth-watering watermelons, and all at a bargain price. On either side of the highway numerous billboards promoting an odd assortment of modern products greet us. A Coca Cola billboard stands alongside an advertisement for Pepsi Cola, as if to underline that both brands can live as peacefully next to each other as can the various religions. And towering above them is a recently painted poster warning of AIDS and encouraging those, who find it difficult to remain faithful to their partners, to use condoms or "zero graze", a local term for fidelity.

Birds in all colours and sizes fly lazily in the cloudless blue sky. Outcrops of hilly tops on a background of green savannah engender a feeling of moving through paradise. Ugandan soil, as the English statesman Sir Winston Churchill aptly observed, bursts with scenic vegetation. "The Pearl of Africa" is what Churchill called this equatorial country. But amidst all this abundant richness, suffering and misery are not too far away. As if to underscore the hardship of life in the country we pass a funeral procession led by a bicycle carrying a corpse wrapped in a papyrus mat. "Possibly an AIDS victim," remarks our driver in a casual matter-of-fact manner.

As in so many other African countries, AIDS is the scourge of this country and has claimed the lives of more than one million Ugandans, creating a staggering number of orphans. But the future is not all gloomy. In the crusade against AIDS is the candid straight-talking Mr. Yoweri Museveni, the president of Uganda. Unlike many other African leaders, who prefer not to talk about AIDS in the mistaken belief that rich western tourists would be scared to come on safari or bathe in their oceans and lake resorts, Museveni has openly admitted that the country has a major AIDS problem on its hands. "Sexual laxity existing today is a colonial phenomenon," he once commented, "We have lost the traditional values, and yet we do not have a sophisticated health network of the modern world." It is this kind of openness, and much more besides, which has helped Uganda register a decrease in the number of new AIDS cases, particularly among its young population[3].

Thirty minutes of driving bring us to Mbalala, our final destination. On the left side of the road we get our first glimpse of the corrugated iron roofed church with walls painted in blue and white. Bougainvillaea in red, blue and purple colours arch over the entrance. A broad smiling smartly dressed lady in a colourful chiffon *busuti*, a dress fastened by a broad sash that goes all the way down to the ground with a long delicate sweep, welcomes us. The *busuti* is the traditional dress for Ugandan women and is supposed to look best on generous bottoms. We explain to the woman that we are here to talk to the pastor. We will have to wait, she says, because the pastor is still delivering the Sunday sermon. "It is a Sunday today," our kindly hostess reminds us. "And it's a special Sunday," she generously adds. We are informed it is Prophet Elijah's birthday.

After a twenty-minute wait the faithful came streaming out of church. If dressing is a good indicator of social status, and there is reason to believe that this holds as true in Uganda as elsewhere, then the adherents were people of varying means. Some of them were evidently as poor as the proverbial church mouse and others were so richly dressed they could rival medieval bishops.

Finally it was time to meet the pastor – or rather the prophet as his followers refer to him. If your idea of a prophet is an austere-looking man wearing a sackcloth and with a dirty beard and long matted hair then we must disappoint you. The prophet was clad in a double-breasted white suit with white shoes to match. He reminded us of a pop star about to start his performance. And his mannerisms were most civil and refined. He listened attentively, rather like a father to his unreasonable children. We had travelled all the way from Kampala because we wanted to know a bit more about the origins of this miraculous church and its message to mankind. He answered all our questions and even invited us to tea.

This is how it all started. As a young minister of a Pentecostal church at a nearby dusty town he had often asked himself why miracles weren't as common in our times as in the days of the Old Testament. It is thus that he resorted to prayer, meditation and fasting in order to get to the core of this fundamental question. After a few months of this intense regime, God finally answered his prayer. In the quiet of the night he heard a fluttering of wings and lo and behold! There on the end of his bed sat the Archangel Gabriel. Gabriel announced that the pastor's wife had been chosen to bear a child who would prepare the world for the Second Coming of Jesus, the

Son of God Almighty. The child was to be known as Malachi and would be one and same as Elijah. At this point the pastor referred us to Malachi 4:5-6 where the birth of this child was supposedly prophesised many centuries ago: "But before the great and terrible day of the Lord comes, I will send you the prophet Elijah. He will bring fathers and children together again; otherwise I would have to come and destroy your country."

Undoubtedly, the pregnancy was characterised by innumerable miraculous acts. On numerous occasions the child spoke with the parents while still in the womb. Delivery was not at the local hospital because the Archangel had explicitly warned the pastor against committing his wife to the care of human midwives. Instead armies of heavenly angels consisting of the very best in midwifery descended upon the pastor's humble dwelling and assisted the mother in bringing forth the precious little Elijah. Those who are familiar with the Bible will recall that the biblical Elijah was male and when reading the aforementioned verses in Malachi, they are inclined to think that the new Elijah must be male. Misrepresentation of biblical truth, says the pastor. Gender was not discussed in those particular verses and Elijah could be female as well. The pastor shook his head in apparent impatience with obdurate mortal humans of flesh and blood, patently incapable of understanding the mystical ways of God. He then quoted yet another scripture text, Isaiah 55:8-11. "My thoughts," says the Lord, "are not like yours, and my ways are different from yours. As high as the heavens are above the earth, so high are my ways and thoughts above yours." Indeed, the Elijah in Mbalala is female and there is no mystery about it particularly if you are able to understand the aforementioned quotation from Isaiah. And how blessed we were, the prophet told us, to visit on that particular Sunday when Elijah's birthday was being celebrated. We did not have the opportunity of meeting her, but we were informed that in spite of lacking a formal education she knew the Bible far better than her learned father.

She preached once a year and the rest of the time she spent in the company of angels, who prepared her for the ultimate mission of winning people back into God's fold before the final battle with the great Satan. "You might be wondering why God has decided to lead his people from Uganda," the prophet put it to us. Yes, we were curious, and we were sure we were not alone. He opened the Bible again and referred us to Isaiah, this time quoting verses from chapter 19. "I will hand the Egyptians over to a tyrant, to a cruel king who will rule them. I, the Lord Almighty, have spoken," he recited with a satisfied smile.

We pointed out that the verse was in reference to Egypt and there had been no mention of Uganda. "Precisely," said the prophet exuberantly, "therein lies the catch. The Bible should not be interpreted literally. Remember Isaiah 55:8-11?" He went on to explain that Egypt was really a biblical metaphor for Uganda and the dictator referred to was none other than Idi Amin, the butcher who ruled Uganda from 1971 to 1979. Ugandans recall how he threw opponents in the crocodile infested River Nile causing the water to stink of decomposing human flesh. That too was prophesised, according to the prophet, quoting the relevant Isaiah text: "The channels of the water will stink as they slowly go dry."

But the girl, we persisted, how did she fit into the picture? The prophet counselled patience; he was not yet through with Isaiah 19. "When that time comes, there will be an altar to the Lord in the land of Egypt and a stone pillar dedicated to him at the Egyptian border. They will be symbols of the Lord Almighty's presence in Egypt. When the people there are oppressed and call out to the Lord for help, he will send someone to rescue them." Wow, interesting stuff, we agreed. Our only regret was that we were unable to meet the rescuer, who was quite busy, in the presence of angels, charting strategy in the coming confrontation with evil. By the way, in case you were wondering what became of the original biblical Covenant Box symbolising the pact between God and his people, well, it is in the girl's room where it is guarded by an angel brandishing a sharp two-edged golden sword.

The story of this Mbalala prophet and his daughter may sound ridiculous to many an ear, but not to the thousands who follow the cult zealously and believe its teachings. The ***Covenant Box Descended into Uganda*** is not the only Christian church active in Uganda claiming to derive its existence from a spiritual experience involving direct communication with God or other heavenly beings. People like the prophet of the ***Covenant Box*** are law-abiding citizens who operate within the limits of the law. Their messages and pronouncements might come across to non-adherents as being on the fringes of sanity but the vast majority of the millenarian groups in Uganda do not display any violent streak. However, a few cults in Uganda have made violence a trademark. Perhaps one of the best known Uganda cults in the past years is the ***Holy Spirit Movement*** of Alice Lakwena and the ***Lord's Resistance Movement*** of Joseph Kony.

Alice Auma, also popularly called Lakwena, was a young Ugandan woman who emerged in the northern district of Gulu around September 1987[4] . She promised to lead the people of that district in an insurrection that would defeat Uganda's president, Yoweri Museveni, and his ruling National Resistance Movement (NRM). She could do this, she claimed, because she was under the control of two powerful spirits; the Holy Spirit and the ghost of an Italian who had worked and died in a northern Ugandan town sometime around the beginning of the twentieth century.

At the time of Lakwena's emergence, much of northern Uganda resented Mr. Museveni who, a year earlier, had overthrown a government dominated by ethnic groups from northern Uganda. Lakwena managed to put together a ragtag army of six thousand soldiers. Each of the fighting men and women were anointed with butter oil, which, Lakwena claimed, had the capacity to deflect any bullet fired by government soldiers.

Besides the bullet-proof qualities of butter oil, the Lakwena movement (officially known as ***Holy Spirit Mobile Force***) instructed its soldiers to attack government troops using rocks and sticks. These, it was promised, would have a magical effect upon reaching their target; they would explode with the devastating force of bombs. Armed with these beliefs Lakwena's army appeared to be superior to the well-equipped Kalashnikov-carrying government troops. Lakwena's forces marched southwards, registering a series of brilliant victories. They routed government soldiers from almost all places in northern Uganda and finally entered eastern Uganda, to the horror of many a terrified Ugandan. Finally they came within the vicinity of the River Nile, and were poised to make the final dash for Kampala, the seat of government.

The only obstacle that seemed to stand between them and the capture of Kampala was the mighty River Nile. Government troops were planning their last line of defence on the western banks of the river. The big question at the time was how Lakwena and her army would cross the River Nile, since rumour had it that government was planning to destroy the only crossing at the Owens Falls dam in order to thwart her advance. No problem, declared a confident spirit-possessed Alice Lakwena. Like the biblical Moses she would strike the waters of the Nile with her staff and the waters would part.

When government troops caught wind of this military strategy there was near pandemonium within their ranks. Before she could venture as far as the Nile, Lakwena and her army were surrounded some one hundred and twenty kilometres east of Kampala. The prophetess managed to escape but thousands of her followers were killed.

With the defeat of Lakwena, one Joseph Kony, a distant cousin of hers, who worked as a Catholic lay catechist, claimed to have inherited her spiritual powers. He preached that the Holy Spirit had given him the mandate to overthrow the southern-dominated Museveni government violently and establish a new state where the Ten Commandments of God would be strictly observed. He formed the ***Lord's Resistance Movement*** that recruited people forcibly in its ranks. Over the years this movement has subjected northern Uganda to extreme violence. Children have been abducted and brutalised, girls and women raped. The ones the ***Lord's Resistance Movement*** did not kill were mutilated; ears, noses and limbs chopped off[5] .

Apart from these radical cults, which practised an extreme form of violence to achieve secular goals, a few other Ugandan cults have come under scrutiny for suspected violations of human rights. Although they are few, the most interesting is a group that was led by Wilson Bushara.

In September of 1999, six months before the infamous Kanungu cult condemned over one thousand of its followers to a violent death, a certain Wilson Bushara, a leader of a group calling itself the ***Last Message Warning Church*** assembled almost one thousand of his followers in a little central Ugandan village. Bushara preached that the end of the world was only three months away, on the eve of the new millennium. Only the righteous would proceed to heaven, and their number he could count on his fingers. For the sinners, however, all was not lost. There was still room to get a good and secure place in heaven instead of hell, where their group rightly belonged. All it required was to purchase a ticket to heaven.

Tickets to heaven could be bought from the prophet very much in the manner that one buys a cinema or concert ticket. Many sold their earthly possessions and handed the money to prophet Bushara. Afraid that she might end up in hell at the turn of the millennium, one young lady stole and sold off 100 cows, just to raise the necessary money for assured comfort in heaven[6] .

Bushara also preached that followers share their wives, a doctrine he referred to as "brotherhood". If this sounds odd, then one only needs to look at the cultural background of most of the followers of this cult. All cult members were from western Ugandan ethnic groups where father in-laws are entitled to sexual intercourse with their daughters-in-law and sharing of wives amongst brothers is an accepted norm[7] . Therefore, by falling back on traditional precedent, it was a relatively easy matter for the prophet to enforce and live his bigger fantasies. Unfortunately, his fantasies also included sleeping with minors whom he took by force, and that was no small offence.

Bushara was also accused of training a private army on his farm and there were charges of regular abduction of children levelled at him. Most African governments would not mind so much about the latter. It is the former, more than anything, which most likely led the government to instruct police to disband the group. In reference to Bushara and his activities, a journalist writing in the government owned newspaper, the *New Vision*, warned rather prophetically, "The last thing little poor Uganda needs on her endless plate of problems is an avalanche of problems from bloodthirsty cults."

When police stormed Bushara's camp they discovered eighteen shallow graves, believed to be those of children who had died under mysterious circumstances at the hands of the cult. This finding did shock the country and some people began wondering if it wasn't about time that the government put a ban on millenarian groups. On 17th March 2000, a Catholic cult calling itself the ***Movement for the Restoration of the Ten Commandments of God***, with its headquarters in the remote area of Kanungu, in western Uganda, would make Bushara and his cult look like a bunch of good-natured smiling clergy. The events shook the little village to its foundations and no-one who witnessed the madness will ever be the same again.

Kanungu should not have come as a surprise to observers of the Christian church in Uganda. With all sorts of Christian groups mushrooming every other day and each claiming to be completely different from any other by introducing a slight variation on a primary theme, it was all too clear that sooner or later, some charismatic, overzealous spiritual leader would be struggling to perform Christian rites in a rather different and original way; perhaps by literally baptising followers with fire.

Chapter 2
Apparition mania

Then a great and mysterious sight appeared in the sky. There was a woman, whose dress was the sun and who had the moon under her feet and a crown of twelve stars on her head. Revelation 12:1

Before that fateful day on 17th March 2000 the average Ugandan walking the streets of Kampala had never heard of Kanungu, and those who had, dismissed the place as an insignificant township in the backwaters of rural Uganda. People we spoke to could not remember any major news event unfolding in Kanungu worthy of national coverage. It was an obscure place in the south-west region of the country.

When you take the bumpy, dusty trail from Rukungiri, a medium-sized city, you are likely to drive the entire way to Kanungu without coming across another vehicle. You will see endless mounds of giant red anthills lining the road and a green mountainous landscape. Occasionally you come across young lads grazing large herds of long-horned Ankole cattle in the lush green pastures. These are Bahima pastoralists, a group ethnically close to the Tutsi of Rwanda, and whose love for cattle is legendary. You will see peasants, mostly women, working the fields in the hot tropical heat. On both sides of the road are coffee fields, banana plantations and acres of maize, which speak for a fertile countryside. In fact, the region is so fertile and blessed with such good weather that it is possible to grow crops throughout the year.

The town of Kanungu has a few thousand people, most of whom are peasant farmers of Bairu stock, a people ethnically related to the Hutu of Rwanda. Life in Kanungu village with its mud and wattle huts, nestling in the enchanting hills of south-western Uganda, was so mundane that even the most vivid stretch of the imagination couldn't bring one to consider the place as a likely candidate for a bizarre mass suicide. But perhaps it is precisely because it is so unremarkable that the doomsday cult, the ***Movement for the Restoration of the Ten Commandments of God***, chose it as their headquarters.

When we drove into the village centre, eager locals, advising us enthusiastically on tourist attractions in the region, mobbed our car. "Want to see mountain gorillas?" a friendly man inquired as he pointed to a hilly area southwards. And not far off are the stupendous Virunga volcanoes. We had had the opportunity of seeing them in their entire glory a day before. They were a breath-taking sight, towering into the clear blue sky. Quite often the mist obliterates the volcano chains. The Virunga volcanoes lie in the neighbouring country of Rwanda and are home to the rare mountain gorillas. It was somewhere out there in the usually misty mountains that Dian Fossey, an American occupational therapist, lived amongst the gorillas for almost twenty years defending them against poachers. While Rwandans were still celebrating Christmas in 1985, her lifeless body was found in her cabin at Karisoke. She had been murdered[8] .

When news of Hutu militias massacring Tutsis and moderate Hutus in Rwanda reached Kanungu in 1994, there was a general air of disbelief. Of that period, which left over one million people hacked to death, one man, a retired court clerk, remarked, "The devil had been set loose in that country, turning father against son and mother against daughter. I knew a Hutu man, a court clerk to boot, who killed his own children because they had been brought into the world by a Tutsi wife. And to think that they had been married for twenty-three years is to appreciate the extent to which the devil manipulates humans." Was it really the great Satan or the weakness of man? "Oh yes, my dear good friends, it is only Lucifer who is capable of conjuring up such plots," said the man, shaking his white-haired head. Then he went on, almost in a whisper, to narrate the story of the vision in Kibeho, a village in Rwanda.[9]

Since the conversion of the majority of its population to Catholicism in the early twentieth century, Rwandans observed the catechism prescribed by their new faith like no other in the region. The central role that God played in Rwandan society was appreciated so much by King Mutara III Rudahigwa that he consecrated the country to Jesus Christ. That was in 1946, when European missionaries were still labouring to convert other African countries to Christianity.

Besides the undisputed role of Christ as King and Saviour, most Rwandans gave the Virgin Mary a special place of prominence in their worship. Calendars of the Madonna and Child hanging alongside the portrait of the head of state adorned almost every Rwandan home, at least they did before the genocide of 1994. Sometime in 1981 a prominent Italian member of an international Marian movement visited the Catholic country of Rwanda. He prophesied that in the coming times, and in a not too distant future, the Virgin Mary would perform miracles in that country. This pronouncement filled many with fear and anticipation, and the country became alive with talk of the soon-to-come miracles. This prophesy was repeated by Catholic priests from the pulpit, and schoolchildren discussed and debated the nature of the approaching wondrous deeds. Even in the marketplace talk was about the predictions of the revered Italian Marian. The country was ripe for a miracle. The seed had been sown…

In the village of Kibeho there was a Catholic secondary boarding school. In 1981, one of the students, fifteen-year-old Alphonsine Mumureke, was going about her daily chores when she was suddenly jolted out of her thoughts by a voice calling her, "*My child.*" She turned in the direction of the voice, which seemed to be floating above her head. What she saw was a beautiful dark-skinned woman dressed in white robes and a white veil. She introduced herself as "the Mother of the Word." Elated, Alphonsine ran to her dormitory to relate to the other girls her encounter with the Virgin Mary.

Of course, most didn't believe her, but not everyone at school was sceptical. The believers prayed day and night for the revelation of the apparition to another student. If this were to happen, they believed, it would confirm Alphonsine's spiritual experience. In May 1982, Marie-Claire Mukangango had her own encounter with the Virgin Mary. Mary appeared to her and spoke thus, "*I ask you to repent. If you say the rosary and meditate on it, you will have the strength to repent. Today many people do not know how to ask for pardon. They put Jesus on the cross again. I wish to remind you of this above all in Rwanda so that I can find humble people who are not attached to riches and money. There is not much time left for you to let yourself be distracted by the gods of this world.*"

The second Kibeho apparition convinced even the sceptics, of whom there were quite a sizeable number. Many students started praying in the hope of experiencing an apparition. By coincidence, two other female students were fasting, as is quite common in Catholic communities. In the middle of the fast, which had lasted eight days in the case of Agnes Kamagaju, Jesus appeared to her and said, "*I come to this Earth but people do not understand. They are amused. Tell them to talk to me directly and I will listen to them. I have come to prepare the way for your good, and you do not understand. There isn't much time left and your attention is focused elsewhere.*" To the other girl, Anathalie Mukamazimpaka, the Virgin Mary supposedly said, "*How long are you going to be deaf to my calls? I love you, my sweet child. Do you love me?*"

Another wonderful miracle, it is claimed, was experienced by a young Muslim lad. Jesus is said to have visited this young boy on several occasions. During their conversations Jesus managed to squeeze in time to teach him all about Christianity and he became so good in his catechism that within a few months he was baptised. Preparing for baptism in most African countries is a process that usually takes years.

During one of their conversations Jesus told him, "*Poverty is not the lack of sweet potatoes to eat. Poverty is to be deprived of the grace that leads us to the Lord. True riches are the riches of the heart. We run after the goods of this earth ... we run after the wind. On this earth we are all poor. We have need of the gifts of God. The goods of this earth are cinders. We cannot present ourselves in front of God with our treasures.*" When the young man, now baptised Emmanuel, asked Jesus about the time of his Second Coming, this is what the Lord supposedly said, "*You will know my Second Coming is at hand when you see the outbreak of religious wars. Then, know that I am on the way.*" The apparitions, it is claimed, appeared to more girls and boys in Kibeho village.

Such accounts undoubtedly led many to believe that there was something spiritually divine in this Rwandan village. Villagers and pilgrims from all over the country, even some from neighbouring Uganda, soon began gathering outside the local Kibeho church to see the seers communicating with Jesus and the Virgin Mary. There was much singing, dancing and praying[10] . Pilgrims often claimed to see miraculous signs spread out in the sky like a painting on canvas. On more than one occasion pilgrims reported seeing the sun veer away from its normal course and spin in the heavens.

Others saw the sacred heart, and some reported seeing the monstrance and its sunburst edges wheeling across the skies. In August 1982, while most of the seers were hoping for an apparition, it is claimed that the Virgin Mary appeared. She was deeply disturbed and on more than one occasion wept bitterly as she showed them disturbing images of a future to come. The images were of apocalyptic proportion. Rwanda had been watched from up above and been found wanting on most accounts. The nation of Rwanda and her people would be subjected to a great catastrophe of a degree as yet unknown to mankind because of her transgressions. Thousands upon thousands would perish, and brother would turn against brother, and sister against sister. The sound of machetes would be heard scything across the hills as throats were slit and bellies ripped open. Cries of mothers and fathers would echo from Kigali to Butare. No place would be safe and no family spared. The seers were shown rivers of blood and a desolate country. The entire land was embroiled in a state of general mayhem, the likes of which had never been visited upon Mother Earth. However, recommitting Rwanda to Christian values through declaring a period of national repentance and prayer would remove the spell of disaster to come. Many more people in Kibeho and the surroundings claimed to have received visions of Jesus or the Virgin Mary soon after the public manifestation of the miracle of the sun, and in most cases they were allowed a glimpse of the looming apocalyptic convolutions.

It wasn't long before events that seemed to have been prophesised unravelled in a most macabre manner. It seemed as if the devil had indeed been set loose in Rwanda during the summer of 1994. In churches, schools and in houses, Tutsi and moderate Hutu were slaughtered by *interahamwe*, a ragtag paramilitary organisation of bloodthirsty monstrous men and women, who traversed every corner of the country, flushing out their prey. Machetes were the preferred instruments of execution. When it came to chopping off heads or slicing bellies of pregnant women, their speed and efficiency in exterminating the innocent and defenceless is unparalleled in human history. Swollen bodies in all states of decomposition littered streets and public parks throughout Rwanda. In Uganda, along the shores of Lake Victoria, thousands of bodies that had been thrown in River Kagera were washed ashore: four thousand at the final count. Some had limbs amputated and eyes gorged out. They were men, women and children of all ages.

In Kibeho, where the seers had experienced their apparitions outside the local church, frightened Tutsi (mostly women and children) sought refuge and protection inside the house of worship. But the *interahamwe* bandits soon caught up with them. In one of the most ruthless and satanic manifestations of the 1994 genocide in Rwanda, over twenty thousand people were slaughtered inside the compound of Kibeho church[11] . Among the dead were twenty-two clerics of the Roman Catholic Church.

The bitterest irony of this tale lies in the fact that the local bishop who had been so convinced by the authenticity of the apparitions in the 1980s was charged as an accomplice in the Kibeho massacres. He protested his innocence but the state prosecutor was convinced of the bishop's guilt and pressed for the death penalty. After a slow and long court process, the courts acquitted the bishop of genocide charges in June 2000. There was simply no evidence linking him to the architects of the slaughter. Could it be possible that a nation's preoccupation with apparitions might have driven people to commit hideous crimes in the belief that it was all predestined and God had to use someone to fulfil a prophecy? It is a matter that needs further exploration and is beyond the scope of this book.

The Uganda-Rwanda border is a dynamic boundary (if the two countries are not quarrelling, which happens often). Usually what occurs in either country is known in the other within minutes. It therefore comes as no surprise that Marian enthusiasts in Uganda were well informed of the Kibeho apparitions. Many Ugandans, especially from the western districts that neighbour Rwanda, overcame linguistic barriers and travelled to Kibeho to see the seers with their own eyes[12]. Marian enthusiasts soon started traversing the length and breadth of Uganda but more especially the districts of western Uganda, circulating stories about the Kibeho apparitions and urging sinners to repent before it was too late. As often happens when relating stories to others, the original tale gets so drastically distorted that it becomes a new story in its own right. Some already alleged at this stage that the Virgin Mary had told the Kibeho seers that she would appear in complete glory at the end of the millennium. Some Marian enthusiasts interpreted this to mean the beginning of the end of the world, which inevitably meant tribulations of cosmic proportion. An apparition mania had entered Uganda.

As the Kibeho apparitions were continuing in Rwanda, an eighteen year old girl came to a little village called Mbuye in the backwaters of Rakai, a south-western district of Uganda particularly devastated by the AIDS epidemic[13]. She was called Specioza Munkatabona and she originated from Rwanda[14]. She was a pretty young woman with a smooth charming voice. According to her followers she was pure and devoid of the original sin.

Specioza claimed to be in regular contact with the Virgin Mary, and that the Virgin spoke to the world through her. Specioza called upon Ugandans to repent their sins and renounce their adulterous ways or else they would soon perish. She emphasised in her sermons that God had sent AIDS as punishment for the sins that the people of Uganda were committing. She claimed that the Virgin had promised to hand her a cure for AIDS if people turned away completely from their evil ways.

Specioza was a fiery preacher who could inspire and galvanise a crowd. The congregation cheered and wept openly with joy when in her presence. The spiritually and physically infirm came from all over Uganda in search of healing. In particular it was believed that a nearby stream, where Specioza claimed to have had regular meetings with the Virgin, could heal AIDS. Rumours were rife that hundreds of people had been cured of the dreaded disease after bathing in the stream. It was also widely believed that whenever she went to receive the holy Eucharist the host transformed into the real flesh of Christ, and the wine in her mouth turned into Christ's very blood. Many claimed to have witnessed this miracle on several occasions.

But it didn't take long before her shine began to wear off. People began claiming loudly that she was a fraud, and her so-called miracles a fraudster's trick. Nonetheless Specioza's healing stream is still there in Mbuye and visited by hundreds of devout pilgrims every year. Even to this very day one encounters pilgrims who tell of miraculous experiences after immersion in the holy spring. Specioza's church still stands in Mbuye and the mantle has been passed on to an elderly woman, Sodona Kehuki Kyinkuhaire, of whom more will be said later. The church preaches that the end of the world is nigh, and followers should not place their trust in modern medicine. It also forbids members from eating pork and encourages them to work on the church farm for much of the day.

While Specioza basked in her glory, another woman, Gaudia Kamushwa, claimed to have witnessed a miracle in Nyabugoto, another village in south-western Uganda. She alleged that while taking an evening stroll she had witnessed a rock at a cave entrance transform into the Virgin Mary. She further testified that the Virgin Mary had then instructed her to convert people back to the Lord's teachings. All the sick and burdened would also find healing and solace if they prayed forthwith at the Nyabugoto rock.

Once again people came from near and far to listen to the bearer of a message from heaven. Even some of Specioza Munkatabona's followers from Mbuye deserted their prophetess, choosing to follow the new vibrant voice of Gaudia Kamushwa. She demanded that her followers donate money to support her church's work among the poor. However, it is doubtful if any of the money ever trickled down to the destitute. It is noteworthy that her second-hand clothes business was in financial doldrums before the vision.

Among Gaudia Kamushwa's early converts were two sisters, Credonia Mwerinde and Ursula Komuhangi. The two sisters claimed to be in contact with the Virgin Mary on an almost daily basis as well. These three women likened themselves to the Fatima children of Portugal—three shepherd children who had a vision of the Virgin in 1917. The Fatima miracle had repeated itself in Uganda, they preached. Interestingly, they claimed to be in possession of the third secret of Fatima, which according to them, referred to the disturbing events that would culminate in the end of the world.

When the Virgin Mary appeared to the three Portuguese children she told them three secrets about events that were to happen in the near future. She predicted that the end of World War One and the beginning of the Second World War would each be preceded by a strange light in the sky. Also, the Virgin told the children about the emergence of Russia as a superpower, committed to spreading its erroneous ideology (read communism) throughout the world. But the third secret remained a mystery. The church, which knew about it, was content to let the faithful guess about the nature of this third secret.

Inevitably, church silence on this undisclosed part of the Fatima apparitions gave impetus to an amazing number of theories as scholars and ordinary Mary enthusiasts outdid each other in establishing the exact nature of the secretive message. Most seemed to agree the message predicted approaching wars and persecutions with entire nations becoming annihilated in the process[15] .

Around 1989 the Gaudia cult got a visitor. He bore no resemblance to the New Testament apocalyptic horsemen. He came driving a white Toyota pick-up truck. With him were his wife, Theresa, and two Catholic nuns. The visitors had been alerted in a vision about the sacred teachings of some women who had been blessed with the visions of the Virgin Mary. The man introduced himself as Joseph Kibwetere, a humble servant of God. In his infinite goodness and mercy the Almighty had revealed himself to him as well. Yes, he had seen and talked to the Virgin Mary on several occasions, Kibwetere had said. He even claimed to have recorded the conversations on tape. The earliest of these recordings dated way back to 1984.

The Gaudia group was quite impressed by the man's track record. To them this was a sign that the Virgin was beginning to direct the rich and powerful to a path of righteousness, for Joseph Kibwetere was a respected businessman whose wealth ranked him among the richest in the district. Poor and rich knew the man. When he saw the yawns and hungry looks of the faithful in the Gaudia cult compound he was overcome by great compassion. Man cannot live on the word of God alone: he needs bread too. Unable to multiply a few loaves of bread and fish to feed the multitudes, he reached for his black attaché case and dished out money to the faithful. "A generous soul sending manna to starving folk," that is what they must have thought of him. The people in the Gaudia compound were moved by Kibwetere's generous gesture.

It was during Kibwetere's subsequent visit to the Gaudia group that Credonia claimed Kibwetere's visit to the Gaudia compound had been revealed to her many years earlier by the Virgin Mary, who had shown her a vision in which Kibwetere was the central figure in restoring the Ten Commandments of God. People had sinned and unless they returned to the Lord's commandments, they would perish in a raging fire. Salvation, however, awaited only those who would repent and live according to the Ten Commandments. It must have been music to Kibwetere's ears as he proclaimed that he too had been instructed by the Virgin Mary to lead the faithful back to strict observance of the Ten Commandments. Thus it was decided that for the realisation of this difficult and challenging mission, Credonia had to work hand in glove with Kibwetere. It is then that Credonia and her sister Ursula left the Gaudia group and travelled to the Kibwetere home where the two sisters came to dominate the affairs of that household.

Kibwetere and Credonia travelled to all corners of their home district exhorting people to turn away from their sins and live according to the laws of God as stipulated in the Ten Commandments. Many listened and some were converted. Soon, followers who fervently believed in the coming inferno for those who refused to repent and lead a life governed by the commandments flooded the Kibwetere home.

After months of entertaining sometimes hundreds of unwelcome followers, Kibwetere's wife and children became particularly uncomfortable at this massive invasion of their privacy. It was especially difficult to stomach the fact that Credonia Mwerinde was now the de facto head of the Kibwetere homestead. She demanded total obedience to her and often roughed up the children. Theresa Kibwetere wasn't spared either. She was treated no better than a servant in her own home. On occasion, when she felt like letting off some steam and asserting her new found authority in the Kibwetere home, it is reported that Credonia didn't hesitate to subject Theresa to numerous lashes of the whip. She claimed the instructions to punish Theresa were from the Virgin Mary. With every passing day she became increasingly belligerent, and to make matters worse, Credonia and Ursula decided that it was in the interest of their ministry to share the bedroom with Kibwetere[16]. It seemed nobody could restrain these two sisters; they were free to do whatever they felt like.

Did Joseph Kibwetere permit this to happen with impunity? Well, the man was under the spell of Credonia and lived in awesome fear of her visions. He was at her beck and call.

After months of living in tyranny, one of Kibwetere's sons summoned up enough strength and courage and managed to get rid of the visitors, who had overstayed their welcome. Credonia and Ursula were given an ultimatum to leave and keep their hands off the Kibwetere property or else suffer the consequences of more degrading humiliation. Frustrated and annoyed that his own flesh and blood had failed to see the light burning so brightly in their midst, Kibwetere summoned his family and roundly denounced and disowned them. He wasn't bitter; he was disappointed in his own wife and children. Only those who believed in his divine mission were worthy of being referred to as his family. Credonia Mwerinde and her sister Ursula fitted that definition quite well.

Thus, in 1991, Joseph Kibwetere denounced his wife and children, left the home he had so painstakingly built and off he went with his close associate Credonia. That is how they ended up in Kanungu, where they established a flourishing community living according to their interpretations of the Ten Commandments and prophesying the end of the world at the millennium. They called their organisation the ***Movement for Restoration of the Ten Commandments of God*** and insisted it was not a new religious group. It was a movement embracing all persons, irrespective of faith. During one of her frequent chats with the Lord Jesus Christ, accompanied by the Virgin

Mary on this particular occasion, Credonia Mwerinde claimed to have been told, "*I died on the cross and shed my blood for all, be they Catholic, Muslim or pagans. And this message is for all, irrespective of creed.*"[17]

The message of the movement was to call upon the people of God to return to true religion. This meant observing the Ten Commandments and rejecting all that is evil. Satan was on the loose, marking people with a triple six mark on the forehead or right arm. Further, those marked by Satan would be showered with favours and lots of money. But these favours and wealth were temporary. Satan and his entire entourage would emerge from the underworld and inflict such terrible suffering hitherto unknown to the world. Male devils would rape women, in the process causing excruciating pains indescribable by human words. Female devils in all their ugliness and lust would force males to fornicate with them. Those who would not dare venture outside their homes in the belief that the devils would let them be were completely wrong. Homes would be invaded by voracious devils that would grab food from stoves and tables. Extreme hunger and deprivation is the price that sinners must pay for their transgressions of the Ten Commandments, Kibwetere and Credonia preached. Woe would befall those who did not strictly follow the commandments. According to the group's own accounts, during his regular discussions with the seers in the Kibwetere movement, Jesus Christ had warned that this time round he would show no mercy to those that had transgressed God's laws.

However, all was not lost, the group counselled. There was still enough time to repent and turn to the Ten Commandments. The soul may be willing to turn to true religion by renouncing sin but the flesh was often weak. Such is the nature of mortal man. To avoid being marked with the triple six it was important to seek help from the seers of the movement, for these were the only ones that God had empowered to guide his children through the coming turbulent times. So overwhelming was this message that thousands sought refuge in the movement. By the time the movement leadership sent over one thousand people to a cruel death, membership was said to be somewhere around five thousand. At the helm of the movement were Joseph Kibwetere, Credonia Mwerinde and the Reverend Father Dominic Kataribabo, the chief ideologue of the movement.

Chapter 3
Cult trinity

Through him God gave me the privilege of being an apostle for the sake of Christ, in order to lead people of all nations to believe and obey. Romans 1:5

In Ruguma, the village of Kibwetere's birth, folk remember him as a benevolent and industrious man. None could be found that could give a negative account of Joseph Kibwetere. He completed his teacher's training at St. George's Teachers College in 1955, a time when the winds of political change swept across the African continent with successive African countries throwing off the yolk of colonialism. In Uganda, the pro-independence movement was getting louder and stronger with each passing day.

Two main political groups had emerged on the Uganda political scene; or rather, two antagonistic Christian streams took up the fight to control political power once the British colonial masters had packed their bags. On one hand were the stiff-necked Protestants under the umbrella of the Uganda People's Congress (UPC), derisively referred to by her opponents as the United Protestants of Canterbury and on the other hand, the hard-mouthed Catholics found solace in the Democratic Party (DP). To UPC folk, the acronym DP stood for *Dini ya Papa*, vernacular for "the pope's religion". Abusive language, mudslinging and scandal mongering characterised the campaign for independence.

In all this charged political atmosphere and not being an important political player, Kibwetere took time off to attend to his romantic needs. And so it came to pass that in 1960 he led a certain Theresa to the altar. For better or worse they became husband and wife. Theresa was a beautiful, shy and soft-spoken damsel of quick wit and deep sympathy. The couple became an example of what living in Christian matrimony was all about. There was love, compassion and understanding.

Kibwetere's first appointment was as a schoolmaster in a Catholic school. He also did voluntary work as a lay teacher in the Catholic

Church. As a teacher in a local Catholic school it was inevitable that he became acquainted, on very personal terms, with most of the clergy. There was the occasional ride to the diocesan headquarters and a chat with the bishop. It is around this time that he developed a strong personal friendship with a young priest, Father Dominic Kataribabo.

In 1961 DP won the elections for self-government. It was a great victory for the Catholics. For the first time in Uganda's muddled political waters, victory was theirs. Kibwetere was ecstatic, as he looked five, ten or forty years from 1961. Like many Catholics of his ilk he believed a DP government would lead this landlocked African country to prosperity built on Christian principles of truth and justice. Alas, the euphoria was short lived. The following year the UPC joined hands with a minor but nevertheless important royalist Protestant party. It was a marriage of convenience that guaranteed victory for the two Protestant parties during the 1962 elections for a post-colonial Uganda government. Disillusionment engulfed the Catholic camp. A book-loving educator with a conviction that the newly independent ex-British colony could conquer their seemingly insurmountable problems entirely through the education of her people, a disappointed Kibwetere decided to steer off politics and concentrated on his core business: promoting education in the region. So enthusiastic was he in his determination to see the universal availability of knowledge, he is said to have spent personal money to pay for the education of promising pupils from financially destitute families[18] . Philanthropic gestures of this magnitude are like angels' visits.

What force took possession of Joseph Kibwetere, an initially good-natured, well-meaning man with a manifest sympathy for the plight of the poor, and turned him into a dangerous religious fanatic of evil repute? Could the answer somehow be found in Uganda's history of political turmoil and his frustration with it? When the UPC formed the first post-colonial Uganda government many believed it would follow the democratic principles enshrined in the constitution. But four years after independence it became evident that the UPC party was out to entrench itself in power at any price. The constitution was abrogated and opposition politicians were routinely harassed and imprisoned.

After the violent overthrow of Uganda's constitution in 1966 the next sixteen years witnessed the plundering of the moral, economic and political fabric of Uganda society. The country slid from progress to decay. A succession of murderous dictatorships presided over the country. Freedom of association and worship became heavily curtailed. Citizens lived in fear as gangs of undisciplined soldiers and paramilitaries roamed the countryside terrorising the populace. Woe to you in those days if you were educated! Teachers, doctors, engineers and other professionals were a particular target. Their bodies, throats slit open, were dumped in the numerous forests or fed to the Nile crocodiles. It was murder of a people through terrorism authorised by the state. Kibwetere managed to weather all these storms even under the most vicious of all Uganda leaders to date—the self-styled Field Marshall Idi Amin Dada[19] .

Idi Amin practised all the forms of evil that an African despot is capable of unleashing on a meek and subservient people, with an absorbing and intense relish. At times dressed as a Soviet-era Field Marshall, and at other moments as a machine gun toting mobster, Idi Amin eroded single-handedly the social and economic base of Uganda. State sponsored terrorism became the order of the day. Some citizens were summarily executed and others stripped of their citizenship. The latter fate befell Ugandans of Asian ancestry. In 1972 Idi Amin shared with the nation the contents of a vision he had received in his sleep. God had instructed him to expel all Ugandans of Asian ancestry. And this had to be done within a few months. In spite of appeals by political and religious leaders from around the world, Idi Amin went ahead with his plans to deport Ugandan citizens.

In a sense, this act of ethnic cleansing was the forerunner of more gruesome acts of tribal hatred that were to affect central Africa long after Idi Amin had disappeared from the political scene. Idi Amin was essentially a bully and in the habit of disposing of those he suspected of opposing his stay in power. It was not unusual that he personally fed them to the crocodiles in the Nile. Amin threw real and imagined enemies to the crocodiles with a frequency that some other people pop popcorn into their mouths. To most Ugandans, the man was Satan incarnate. One had to keep a safe distance from Idi Amin lest he gobbled you up or sent you to the numerous torture chambers, the most notorious of which was located in Kampala's posh diplomatic neighbourhood.

During Amin's reign some of Kibwetere's close associates fled the murderous regime, seeking asylum outside the country. Some of these were notable professors and others were bishops. Yet many others were simple peasants being driven off their lands by Amin's henchmen. Uganda had become a very dangerous place and nobody was safe; even Idi Amin's own close lieutenants were routinely rounded up and executed. The optimism, so evident at independence, had turned into resigned pessimism with fundamental human rights abused as a matter of routine, regardless of political stance or religious affiliation. If the people of this once proud society that Churchill described as the "pearl of Africa" ever hoped to live without fear of being murdered in their houses and in the streets, Idi Amin had to go.

The religious prayed for divine intervention to free the country from the despot. But it seemed that God had forsaken them. Idi Amin continued to murder at will. Finally it came to pass that in 1979 forces from neighbouring Tanzania, a country whose northern province Idi Amin had annexed and plundered, overthrew this vicious megalomaniac[20].

With Idi Amin the mean-spirited buffoon gone so was the fear that had gripped Ugandans during his rule. Ugandans could once again get their hopes up. There was a new breed of politicians on the Ugandan political scene. A new bunch of Ugandan leaders, well educated and generally believed to be democratic, had taken political control. During their years of exile in western capitals, most of the new breed politicians had gained knowledge into how democracies function, or so the populace desperate for better tidings forced itself into believing.

After years of no experience with electing their leaders, the people were told that a general election would soon be organised. And guess what: it would be free and fair! Not many African countries had ever organised such an election, and Uganda was hoping to celebrate her re-entry into the community of democratic nations by holding a free ballot. “We want ballots not bullets” posters hung on walls and tree trunks. Old political parties were resurrected, and so was the sectarian divide. Catholics lined up behind the Democratic Party while Protestants identified themselves with the Uganda People’s Congress. From the pulpit, priests urged their congregations not to betray the faith by casting their vote to politicians of rival Christian denominations. It was during these elections that Kibwetere agreed to use his influence in supporting a Catholic candidate for the Ntungamo parliamentary seat. Onto the campaign trail he went carrying modest posters with a great message of hope: “Vote the Democratic Party for Peace and Justice.”

Though the 1980 national elections were fraught with accusations of voting irregularities and rigging the count to grant victory to the Protestant party (UPC), an international team of election observers declared that “under the circumstances, the elections were free and fair.” Opposition parties cried foul and called for the election results to be annulled, but the electoral commission took no notice, insisting the exercise had been conducted in a most democratic manner. Many were disappointed. So was Kibwetere. It is thought that Kibwetere’s candidate actually won the election but the electoral commission (which clearly favoured the Protestant party) denied him victory.

The UPC had barely formed a government when its functionaries embarked on a systematic program of harassing those who belonged to other parties. Kibwetere was not spared either. Secret police operatives were out to arrest and, most probably, murder him. It was history repeating itself all over again. The dark ages of the Amin era had descended on the country again. People subscribing to political beliefs which were different from the ruling UPC were no longer safe in Uganda. After much soul-searching and extensive consultations with his family and circle of friends, he decided the best thing to do was to go underground. Exile it had to be; but it would be within Uganda. Kibwetere found a place where he could blend into the local populace and live like a pauper, posing no threat to the UPC government.

Given the age-old suspicion between Catholics and Protestants in Uganda, it is interesting to note that it was the Protestant bishop of the neighbouring district of Kabale who gave sanctuary to Kibwetere in his hour of great need[21]. Throughout the rule of the UPC government, which spanned a period of six years, Kibwetere lived in the bishop's compound where he kept a low profile. He made sure that he never attracted attention to himself lest the secret police sniff him out. This was a long and lonesome period in Kibwetere's life, but also one of intense personal and spiritual reflection. He didn't dare visit his home. Interaction with his wife and sixteen or so children was done clandestinely.

Exile had been forced upon him by weaknesses in human systems. Kibwetere saw constitutional government, particularly in Africa, as an illusion. And the problems of the continent would remain as long as men with guns continued to dictate politics. How long would these violent and undemocratic forces haunt Africa? A casual look at the African continent cast a gloomy prognosis. Violence would hang around for a long time to come. It became clear to Kibwetere then, that without some degree of direct divine intervention, Uganda and Africa were set to destroy themselves. War, disease and famine ruled sub-Saharan Africa; it was a ubiquitous picture of despair. However, if the populace prayed, the loving and forgiving heavenly father could look upon Ugandans with mercy and save them from destruction.

As if in partial answer to Kibwetere's prayers, 1986 saw Yoweri Museveni's rag-tag guerrilla force capture power in Kampala after waging a six-year protracted war in the bushes and jungles of central Uganda. There is an old African saying, "When two elephants fight it is the grass that suffers". Hundreds of thousands are believed to have died during the guerrilla insurgency—innocent civilians caught between government troops and Museveni's guerrillas. Finally, the guerrillas prevailed and formed a new government. Just like Joseph Kibwetere, Yoweri Museveni and most in his government originated from western Uganda. This event marked the end of Kibwetere's exile and an extremely spiritual Kibwetere returned home.

Amidst the welcome celebrations he revealed even greater news.

On 25th April 1984 Jesus Christ and the Virgin Mary had appeared to him in exile, anointing him to lead others on a pilgrimage to restore the Ten Commandments that the Almighty had handed down to Moses in the Sinai desert. But how was he going to spread this message? One thing was clear to him: the Catholic Church was hardly the right institution to rely on in spreading this message of monumental import. Another channel to carry out the instructions received in the vision had to be sought. For years he didn't make much headway in spreading the message. It was a message he shared with his family and close friends. However, all this was to change when Kibwetere met Credonia Mwerinde.

Any attempt to understand the forces that motivated Kibwetere cannot be complete without looking at the man's mental state. Kibwetere was known to suffer from psychosis for which he received treatment in Kampala. According to a consultant psychiatrist at Makerere University, he had delusions of grandeur. Now and again he felt he was a terribly important person with clear instructions to lead the world away from destruction. So convinced was he of the ideas that filled his mind and came to preoccupy much of his time that people not familiar with psychotic patients could easily believe the man's conviction. By the time the religious movement murdered its followers, Kibwetere had apparently gone for months without medication. It is instructive to note that Makerere University psychiatrists had already made an observation that quite a sizeable number of people with psychotic illness also had a history of belonging to a cult at one time.

When Dominic Kataribabo's parents deemed the time ripe for the young man to start school they turned to their eldest son Hariseni Oworyanawe, a carpenter, for financial support. Although happy as a carpenter in Mbarara, Hariseni was convinced that if he had had the opportunity to continue with school he might have achieved greater things in life. Perhaps he could have turned out as a lawyer, or even a priest. But it was the financial shortcomings of his parents that conspired to deny him the necessary education.

Secondary education did not come cheap. It required payments of exorbitant school fees—money the family could not dream of ever getting. The family was as poor as the mice that scurried about in their Rugazi village church, which was an affair of cow-dung plastered walls with no window panes. In the church, one was more likely to encounter snakes and other beasts that crawl than the peace normally associated with a house of prayer. Instead of pursuing bigger dreams, Hariseni had to make do with the free vocational training offered by the kindly Catholic missionaries. That is how he ended up training as a carpenter.

His dream, however, was to see one of his siblings go on to get a college education. Therefore when the young Dominic stood at the door of his Mbarara house one day in February 1949, he saw in him the possibility of fulfilling a long cherished dream.

And Kataribabo did not disappoint. He chose the long and tough study that prepares aspiring young men for a celibate career as Roman Catholic priests. Kataribabo was an exceptionally bright man who scored distinctions in most of the subjects at the seminary. Of his days at Katigondo Major Seminary, an old classmate (who failed to make it to Holy Priesthood) recalls, "Dominic was gifted with a photographic memory. Whereas most of us saw spots in the sun during Latin classes, Dominic was thoroughly at home with the ancient language." And his abilities were not only limited to acquisition of archaic Church languages. He was first in the class when it came to scholastic philosophy or dogmatic and moral theology. He also earned a distinction in Canon Law—the set of rules and regulations that govern the Catholic Church. After eight years of hard study at the Major Seminary, Dominic was ordained priest in 1957 and joined a long line that stretches as far back as Christ's disciples in the first years of Christianity. On the day of his ordination, villagers remember the face of a young newly consecrated priest, exuberant in his new responsibility and singularly motivated with a conviction to get out among the tribes of western Uganda, baptising them in the name of the Father, the Son, and the Holy Spirit.

The ordination took place in Rugazi and was quite an occasion. The feast that followed the ordination mass was an almost carnival-like affair and would dominate talk in Rugazi and the immediate environs for many years to come. Food and drink were aplenty. It was as if the miracle of the five loaves and two fishes had been replicated. The drinking fraternity must have been reminded of the miracle of the wine in Cana. For on that day beer aficionados drank to their fill; ale flowed endlessly like the waters of the Nile on their long journey to the Mediterranean. In short, it was a feast befitting one of the first sons of Rugazi to be consecrated into the mysteries of the royal priesthood of the Roman Catholic Church.

Although there was lots of food and drink the partying could not last forever. It was only natural that Father Dominic Kataribabo should embark on his duties of attending to the spiritual needs of the flock entrusted to him. He held several positions as curate until he finally managed to get his own parish. In 1969 the expatriate missionary diocesan bishop, Jean Marie Ogez, retired to his native France. It was time to look for a successor and preferably one drawn from the growing ranks of indigenous clergy.

Father Dominic Kataribabo was considered to be a strong contender for the position, seen by many as able to offer himself enthusiastically and energetically to the diocese. Besides, he was prayerful and spirit-filled. This was a priest capable of providing administrative leadership and overseeing tough decisions in the diocese. In addition he was widely seen as able to establish personal contacts across the Bairu and Hima castes, turning them away from the worship of the heathen Chwezi gods, a practice considered incompatible with Christianity. And the man himself was ready to be bishop.

Dominic Kataribabo reflected on his accomplishments, comparing them with the achievements of others of similar age and background: it was all the more reason to believe in his worthiness for the bishopric. Besides, he was one of the retiring bishop's favourites. He made it known to his superiors that if given an opportunity to shepherd the flock as their bishop, he would consider it a tremendous opportunity to serve Christ and his pilgrim church on earth.

Kataribabo might have been brilliant but at this point in time he did not have enough academic qualifications to get appointed. To become a bishop of the church often requires a list of impressive achievements from first rank Catholic universities. Apart from his diploma in theology and philosophy, there was little he could present in way of scholastic accomplishments. As a result of this lack of experience in the territory of advanced learning, John Baptist Kakubi was appointed in his stead. Bitter at failing to become bishop, Kataribabo reluctantly accepted a new posting as rector of a minor seminary in Mbarara diocese[22].

It is at the seminary that we begin noticing that underneath the cultivated, intellectual façade of this priest lay a rather malignant character. His impatience with those who were slow to learn was clear to the seminarians. Not only was he a strict disciplinarian, hinging on the autocratic, he was also as rabidly temperamental and unpredictable as an African dictator. One moment he was all jovial and placid, and the next he became sullen and angry. It was amazing how quickly he lost his urbane, cultivated mannerisms to an almost evil ferocity that was way out of proportion to the insulting stimuli. One ex-seminarian noted that Kataribabo was a man who glowed with pleasure at the discomfort of others, especially if they were subordinates. At one point he reportedly expelled an entire class for an act of minor disobedience.

As regards his qualities as a priest attending to the spiritual needs of parishioners entrusted to his care, there were no doubts. Most people who knew Kataribabo talk of a priest who gave excellent pastoral care to his parishioners. A priest who knew him rather well remarked, "Dominic is one priest who drew upon his extensive background in mystical theology to develop a solid and strong spiritual life." One middle-aged man in Rugazi who used to visit Dominic before he joined the ***Movement for the Restoration of the Ten Commandments of God*** says, "Even before drinking a glass of water he would take out his pocket Bible and read from Scriptures. He used to say that just as the body needs food and water, the soul must receive nourishment through reading holy writings. You should attend to the needs of the soul at the very times when you replenish the hungry and thirsty body." And besides, he was a well-recognised authority in exorcism, at least according to the accounts of some.

People who believed they were tormented by evil spirits could always turn to him. It was claimed that he sent devils scurrying for dear life through a rigorous programme of prayer and fasting. He was the kind of priest best suited to a rural village parish where belief in the awesome powers of evil spirits abounded.

To grow further spiritually and perhaps enhance his chances of becoming a Bishop, Father Dominic decided to do a doctorate and acquire that degree that had interfered with his brisk march up the Catholic Church hierarchy.

It was in pursuit of a higher degree that Father Dominic ended up enrolling at the Loyola Marymount University, a prestigious Jesuit College in Los Angeles, where he was described by folks as someone no better or worse than any ordinary priest from a third world country[23]. In Los Angeles Kataribabo found time to do some pastoral work at St. Anthony Church. Babies were brought to him for baptism and he was available to hear confessions from those who had broken the Ten Commandments. He listened to their litany of sins and absolved them in the name of the Father and of the Son and of the Holy Spirit.

With a doctorate in theology, Kataribabo returned to Uganda in 1989, hoping to secure a prestigious appointment as chaplain of St. Augustine's chapel, Makerere University, Kampala. Makerere University is the country's premier institution of higher learning[24]. In clergy circles the opinion is largely held that an appointment as chaplain at St. Augustine is just as good as being named bishop. As a matter of fact some consider the job more challenging than running a diocese, given the concentration of highbrow minds in the university community. Pastoral work in such a community is definitely more challenging and different from a parish in some rural village of western Uganda where up to sixty percent of the population could meet the criteria of illiteracy.

At the university the chaplain continuously encounters parishioners who analyse Sunday sermons critically and question every single word. Besides, a significant proportion of the university community looks at Christianity as an archaic institution whose singular achievement on the African continent was to create fertile ground for colonialism. Debating with Marxist-Leninist intellectuals who eschew organised religion on issues such as the Immaculate Conception or the Resurrection can be trying for a St. Augustine chaplain with a scanty knowledge base.

Kataribabo saw himself as the man for the Makerere University job but chaplain of St. Augustine he was not to be. Instead, he got posted to St. George's Teachers College as chaplain and tutor. Although St. George's trained some of the best primary school teachers in the region, such as the educator Joseph Kibwetere, it was not Makerere University. It was a job that he accepted with reluctance. He would have loved to decline this posting but for the oath of blind obedience to his bishop which he had made at ordination into the royal priesthood.

Before he could get to know the names of his students, the bishop issued Kataribabo with new transfer orders to Rugazi, his home village, and it is in Rugazi, sometime during 1989, that Father Dominic Kataribabo entertained two visitors—Joseph Kibwetere and Credonia Mwerinde. Kibwetere was not a total stranger to Father Dominic. The two men knew each other fairly well. The visitors were concerned about what they referred to as the "decaying process" in the Roman Catholic Church.

The visitors impressed Father Dominic. He was in total agreement with their analysis of the crisis that hovered like a cloud of sin over the Catholic Church. And most importantly, he was especially convinced of how they intended (through direct divine intervention) to renew the Holy Roman Catholic Church. Credonia Mwerinde and Joseph Kibwetere were particularly irked at the constant violation of the Ten Commandments. And it was not only those two that were distressed but so were Jesus Christ and his mother.

Jesus and Mary had already expressed their displeasure with the way Catholic Church business was conducted, and Kibwetere claimed that he had recorded on tape the voices of Jesus and Mary expressing their misgivings. Essentially, Jesus and Mary had given this message to Credonia Mwerinde and Joseph Kibwetere: if Uganda did not reform her immoral ways the Almighty would unleash untold suffering upon her people. It was a timely message in Father Dominic Kataribabo's opinion and together with two other Roman Catholic priests, Father Paul Ikazire and Father Kasapurali, they decided to jump on the Kibwetere-Mwerinde bandwagon of spiritual renewal.

The elderly Father Ikazire, who left the Kibwetere cult in 1994 after a successful career in which he reportedly got numerous apparitions, claimed the priests teamed up with Kibwetere because there was no other way in which to correct the Catholic Church and veer it away from a path of self-destruction. "We felt things were going the wrong way. Our Church was reneging on its commitments to give moral leadership to her flock. There was a desperate need to change the manner in which Church business was being conducted. Joining Kibwetere and Credonia was done for the sake of generating ideas on how to rekindle fire in a dying faith[25]". Thus Father Ikazire justified his decision to join the cult.

Of all the leaders of the ***Movement for the Restoration of the Ten Commandments of God***, Credonia Mwerinde was an oddity. It is claimed that she could hardly read or write, having chosen to drop out of school after four years of primary education. This was not because of a failure on the part of her parents to meet the required school fees. It was not even because of the discriminatory habit of parents in these parts of the world, preferring to educate sons and keeping daughters in perpetual ignorance. This is just the kind of notion one would expect from hard-line traditionalists. But Paul Kashaku, Credonia's father, was a Roman Catholic catechist who believed in giving his children the very best education that Catholic schools could offer. Credonia just thought school was not the thing for her. Learning the alphabet and reciting silly rhymes was just too mundane for her.

Credonia might not have been as pretty as a picture but she had a certain attraction about her. Six times did she enter a matrimonial contract, and six times she broke it. Upright and chaste, she was not. One Kanungu villager said Credonia was "troublesome and cantankerous". At one point she was a strumpet of the first order with the morals of the farmyard. She was in her twenties when she started out as a commercial sex worker. After tiring of the sex trade, Credonia Mwerinde returned to Kanungu, her native village, where she quickly found herself a husband of sorts. Unfortunately this marriage, and the five subsequent ones, ended in an acrimonious divorce. Credonia was not the type to be tied down to the dull and monotonous routine of domestic chores. She was used to dictating her own price and not being answerable to some man with ideas of keeping a woman under lock and key. Between marriages, she ran a pub, specialising in *ntonto*[26]. In Kanungu it is not easy to find a kind word about her.

While Kibwetere wore down his shoes treading the dusty Ntungamo roads and Father Kataribabo shouted himself hoarse from the pulpit all in the name of urging residents to vote for the Catholic party in the 1980 election, Credonia Mwerinde did not have strong convictions on politics or religion. Even so, at first she was active in the local branch of the Democratic Party, distributing pamphlets and recruiting other Kanungu residents into the party. On more than one occasion she addressed huge public rallies. Credonia was distinguished in the art of oratory and working crowds was an activity for which she was well suited. But when the Catholic party lost the election Credonia surprised and disappointed many in Kanungu when she crossed over to the ruling Uganda People's Congress.

In all fairness to Credonia it must be stated here that she was not the only DP member who switched political allegiance. A group of opposition parliamentarians crossed the floor en masse joining the ranks of the ruling UPC. Only a principled few, like Joseph Kibwetere, remained loyal to their political beliefs. And for this, he was greatly admired in the region. The likes of Credonia, once in the ranks of the UPC, were best described as belonging to the ranks of ruling party extremists.

When her brother, John Baptist, lost a couple of teeth in a nasty road traffic accident Credonia seized the opportunity to persecute the opposition DP. She advised her brother to give false testimony to the effect that he had been attacked by a marauding bunch of DP supporters led by the local Kanungu DP party boss.

UPC perceived the Kanungu DP party boss as a great threat and wanted him off the political scene. A reward from UPC party headquarters in Kampala awaited any party faithful who could orchestrate the downfall of the Kanungu DP strongman. Of course the UPC was capable of sending their secret police to murder him or hold him incommunicado in a torture house, which Uganda security referred to with a sense of morbid irony as a "safe house". However, he was a very popular figure respected across the ethnic and political divide, so more civil tactics were called for to deal with this annoying matter. As a result, when Credonia's brother came up with the false accusation UPC functionaries seized their chance. Unfortunately for the UPC, when the matter came up in court the magistrate dismissed it on grounds of inconsistency. The prime witness, Credonia Mwerinde, was found to be unreliable. Her accounts of the events were contradictory. It was a case that was impossible for the prosecution to win, even in a country where the judiciary was not famously known for its independence. Defence witnesses who had been travelling in the same vehicle as John Baptist were produced in court and corroborated the accident account.

Many Kanungu residents were sorely offended that the matter ever came up to court. It was seen as yet another example of blatant mockery of the judicial system in Uganda. And that woman, Credonia Mwerinde, came to epitomise the very heart of evil in Kanungu. It was also difficult for them to trust a woman who could not keep a marriage. Besides, she had tried to poison herself after discovering that her younger sister (not Ursula) had been having an affair with the man that Credonia considered as her rightful and lawful husband at that point in time. Kanungu folk apparently believed committing suicide or the mere threat of making away with one's precious life was too high a price to pay for this particular man—an irresponsible brat who drifted from one job to another and with a distasteful penchant of seducing married women.

Little wonder, then, that when misfortune struck her immediate and extended family, Credonia was blamed for being directly behind it. An interesting account is that of her eldest sister's husband, who was supposed to have had many extramarital affairs. At a loss as to how best to reign in her husband, Credonia's sister approached her for advice. Credonia is reported to have come up with the brilliant idea of administering a potent concoction that would make her sister's husband faithful. Indeed the herbal concoction, an overdose as villagers claim, was given to the unsuspecting victim whereupon he vomited to death.

Other outlandish accusations were levelled at Credonia when she lost a brother and recriminations came flowing again when another brother developed psychiatric problems. A most ridiculous accusation came from a man who operated a local pub. He claimed that Credonia had cast a magic spell on his business and as a result most of his customers had abandoned him. The truth of the matter is that it was unlikely that Credonia was the architect of these and other misfortunes for which she was blamed.

In western Uganda, and indeed much of Africa, it is still difficult for most people to accept that misfortune can be brought about by causes other than witchcraft and sorcery. Poor management of a pub will surely cause a dearth in the usual crowd of revellers. As recrimination against Credonia increased she found herself almost ostracised. Few people were willing to be seen as her associates.

All these tribulations notwithstanding, her sixth marriage to one Eric was on the rocks. A shop and bar owner, Eric was by no means a poor man. He entrusted the bar to the management of Credonia, which was a foolish thing to do. Credonia is reported to have drunk herself silly on numerous occasions and at the height of her inebriation, she was in the habit of inviting all and sundry to have one on the house. Soon Eric's bar, which had been a symbol of pride to the local drinking fraternity, went bust. Credonia's husband was furious accusing her of mismanagement and behaving like a prostitute. Shouting and screaming marathons ensued and these soon came to characterise the marriage.

It was at this point that she began talking to her disappointed husband about visions and messages from the Madonna, beseeching him to sell what remained of his property and dedicate the rest of his life to righteous living. But Eric remained sceptical. As far as he was concerned this Madonna tale was a cock-and-bull story.

Nevertheless, Credonia was determined to give her cynical husband a glimpse of the divine and turn him into a true disciple of her visions of the Madonna and the apocryphal messages therein. She took the battle to their bedroom; there would be no more sharing of the matrimonial bed if Eric didn't agree to go to see the Madonna. Finally he relented and accompanied her to Nyabugoto rock for a rendezvous with the Virgin Mary. But try as he might, Eric could not see the Madonna in the Nyabugoto cave. What followed was a clash between the two over the authenticity of Credonia's divine claims, a disagreement that culminated in an acrimonious divorce sometime in August 1988.

Chapter 4
The seer and the rock

I know a certain Christian man who fourteen years ago was snatched up to the highest heaven (I do not know whether this actually happened or whether he had a vision—only God knows). 2 Corinthians 12:2

It was around seven o'clock in the evening when we ventured towards the caves. Darkness was hurriedly asserting itself over daylight. Barely an hour earlier the sun in all its majesty and beauty had hovered over the hills and valleys of western Uganda. The equatorial night had approached and in the absence of the moon it would soon become pitch dark—as dark as the African jungle. And in the jungle countless creatures patiently awaited the dying of the last rays of light before going about their nocturnal activities.

With onset of the black night the dull monotony of wind swishing through trees and savannah thickets would give way to a lively and noisy clatter of a million crickets and a musical buzzing of countless winged insects. An occasional hollow laugh of a hyena lends an element of excitement to the noisy cacophony that defines nightfall in the jungle. It is a miraculous transformation of nature. And in this wonderfully splendid jungle lay the Nyabugoto rock, a remnant of seismic movements that tore through the region millions of years ago. It is on this rock that Credonia claimed to have had the first nocturnal encounter with both the Virgin Mary and Jesus way back in 1986.

It is plausible that stigmatisation drove Credonia in search of a place where she could be free from all the absurd charges of sorcery. Her home village, Kanungu, had turned hostile to her. Wild charges of sorcery by a large cross-section of folk might also have acted to create ideas that led to divine pretensions. Salvation came in the form of a prophetess, Gaudia Kamushwa. Credonia packed her bags and left for Nyamitanga to join Gaudia whose visions of the Virgin Mary were well known in much of western Uganda. Many had left their homes and dear ones to join Gaudia in her Nyamitanga compound.

Credonia became quite close to Gaudia Kamushwa, which might not be surprising since both claimed to be visited by the Virgin Mary and Jesus Christ on almost a daily basis. Interestingly, although Credonia Mwerinde's encounter with the Virgin Mary and Jesus predated Gaudia's own apparition, this did not make her feel more privileged than her new found friend. Even more curiously, Credonia claimed to have begun receiving visits from the Virgin Mary a few months before the Kibeho apparitions in Rwanda. When challenged as to why she hadn't come out in the open much earlier she fell back to the art of being a mystic, a role she executed so adequately. She claimed the divine worked in mysterious ways and that is why she had been instructed by the Virgin Mary not to utter a single word to a living soul about those encounters. She had to wait for more instructions and would tell her story to a wider audience at a time that the Virgin would choose. Thus after patiently waiting for many years the Virgin Mary and Jesus Christ instructed her to go public with the message.

Of her immediate family the earliest convert was her younger sister, Ursula Komuhangi. Ursula abandoned her secondary education and joined the Gaudia cult. In due course she too was talking to the Virgin Mary and Jesus Christ. Followers of the Gaudia cult felt uniquely blessed. For in their presence were three persons with supernatural gifts.

Hungry for spiritual food people flocked to Nyamitanga from all directions. And it is in this frenzy of searching for a wider and deeper meaning of life that Joseph Kibwetere and wife Theresa met the self-styled seers of Nyamitanga. Because they believed the Madonna had predestined their meeting with Credonia, the Kibweteres felt greatly honoured and privileged to be given that unique opportunity of hosting the sisters Credonia and Ursula in their Ruguma home; and it was in Ruguma, amidst several days of fasting and prayer that the ***Movement for the Restoration of the Ten Commandments of God*** was born.

Joseph Kibwetere became the leader of the group. He was the only one to whom the title "prophet" was given. Other cult leaders, including the ones claiming to be in hourly touch with heaven, were never addressed as "prophets" or "prophetesses". Credonia was referred to as the "programmer" because she was the one who mostly communicated the most recent news from the Virgin. To help Kibwetere with the day-to-day running of the group's business, twelve apostles were appointed.

Appointment of the twelve apostles was done in accordance with instructions from the Virgin Mary and her son Jesus Christ given to one Angelina Migisha, a 42-year old woman[27] . Angelina Migisha claimed to have seen and talked to the Virgin Mary when she was only nine years of age. An aggrieved Madonna had told her of the need to restore the Ten Commandments in order for the world to be saved. Before parting company, the Virgin Mary made her swear an oath not to reveal this encounter to any person until such a time that she would re-appear to her (the same kind of oath that Credonia Mwerinde was asked to swear to).

After a particularly long wait characterised by an itching to share her extraordinary experience and numerous moments of coming to within inches of breaking the covenant of silence but for prayer (you see, the devil is a mischievous chap who derives enormous fun tempting the spiritually idle), the Virgin Mary returned as promised. The day was 28th April 1984. The Madonna had not come alone. Her son Jesus Christ accompanied her. And the Madonna spoke thus, "*You have been chosen to be a model Christian for the nation of Uganda. It is through you that God's Ten Commandments will be restored in this nation. Go out and teach your compatriots about these commandments, and they in turn will be instructed to learn from you.*"

Then Jesus spoke, "*During my first coming, I did select twelve male apostles. But this time things will be done differently because I am working closely with my mother. I will anoint six males and she will anoint six females.*" Further, Jesus defined the roles of the twelve. Their major task was to lead God's people in battle against Satan. They were also given authority to drive out evil spirits as well as power to crush devils irrespective of size or shape. The twelve were also entrusted with the authority to save or damn any soul. Credonia, Ursula and Theresa Kibwetere were among the apostles.

The Roman Catholic priest, Father Dominic Kataribabo, who was fascinated by all this talk of apparitions, was made an apostle too. Of course, as might have been expected, his bishop was hardly amused. According to the bishop, and most of the clergy for that matter, the ***Movement for the Restoration of the Ten Commandments of God*** was a dangerous cult whose teachings were incompatible with the beliefs of the Roman Catholic Church. It was clearly spelled out to Kataribabo that joining the cult ranks was a grievous act. It was to embrace schism, which was a revolt against the true faith as preached by the Roman Catholic Church. On countless occasions the bishop and other prominent Catholic clergy tried to persuade Father Dominic to quit the Kibwetere cult[28] . But his counsel fell on deaf ears. Friends and relatives were dispatched to try and talk him out of it, but he rejected all their pleas for him to return to the Catholic Church.

A respected priest, and a classmate of Kataribabo at the seminary in their spiritually formative years, recalls discussing with him the consequences of his decision not to renounce the cult and return to Mother Church. He warned Dominic Kataribabo that by persisting in his disobedience to the bishop and continuing to function as a priest and member of a spiritually and morally devoid organisation that had all the hallmarks of a cult, he might earn himself an excommunication. An excommunication would mean that he no longer belonged to the community of the true Church of Jesus Christ. He would be far worse than an infidel. "Aren't you scared of being severed from Mother Church's umbilical cord that has nourished your soul and spirit to maturity?" the priest had asked Dominic Kataribabo.

But Dominic Kataribabo was in a militant mood and was more than ready to draw upon his deep knowledge of Church law to justify his actions. He responded by stating that through the act of baptism he had denounced Satan and proclaimed his belief in one God, whose only son, Jesus Christ, was crucified, buried and on the third day rose from the dead. It was an act that gave him the moral authority to call himself a Christian. Through baptism, he had said, he had irrevocably become a Catholic. No ecclesiastical authority, be it the bishop or even the pope, could efface that sacrament. He reasoned that joining the cult did not make him any less a Catholic than, for example, the bishop. And for good measure he had added that excommunication was a hollow gesture. It did not prevent him from administering sacred rites to those who had seen the light and humbled themselves to live according to the Madonna's messages handed to him and his fellow seers.

This friend of Dominic Kataribabo remembers that they had been down this road before. But that was a long time ago as young seminarians poring over Canon Law and arguing Martin Luther's pronouncements on the subject of excommunication. Luther had argued that because the act of excommunication did nothing to deny common spiritual prayers of Mother Church to a Christian, it was a mere external punishment of little spiritual significance. Apparently, the Catholic priest Dominic Kataribabo now shared this view. The priest looked at the determination and conviction in his friend's eyes and it dawned on him that no amount of persuasion or threats could change Dominic Kataribabo's deeply held beliefs. To the cult he belonged and in it he would die.

Father Dominic Kataribabo was confident that, by following Kibwetere, he was doing the right thing. Unable to bring him to his senses there was only one alternative open to the Bishop—to excommunicate the rebel priest from the Roman Catholic Church. The ethical and theological pronouncements of the cult were incompatible with the beliefs of the Catholic Church. Pronouncements of daily visions from the Virgin Mary, also claimed by Dominic Kataribabo, were too much of a good thing for the good old diocesan Bishop. In 1991 Father Dominic Kataribabo was relieved of his duties as a Catholic priest and expelled from the Church.

In theory, the consequences of excommunicating a priest come down to this: if the said rebellious priest was to walk into a Catholic Church during mass the presiding priest would be required to stop in the middle of the sacred rite and politely request him to leave the premises immediately. For the heretic no longer belonged to the community of true believers, having made the choice of his own free will and in full command of his mental faculties. And should the excommunicated priest obstinately disobey the order to leave, choosing to remain seated in his pew, then more forceful, arm-twisting tactics had to be employed.

With excommunication, Kataribabo's fate as a Roman Catholic priest was sealed. No more would he ever partake in the common spiritual blessings, which through conformity to Church teaching, are bestowed upon the society of believers in the Roman Catholic Church. But this did not bother him in the least. Kataribabo willingly quit his parish house in Rugazi and pitched his tent at the Kibwetere home, just like numerous other cult members. But he didn't completely quit the village of his birth, Rugazi. He built a private mansion on one of its most picturesque hilltops with a superb view of two volcano lakes and lush terraced valleys. It was a 10-bedroom affair, which, in surroundings dominated by traditionally built grass-thatched huts, was an intimidating and imposing showpiece of fine architecture. The ***Movement for the Restoration of the Ten Commandments of God*** used this premises as one of its numerous so-called "learning centres".

At first Theresa Kibwetere willingly accepted Credonia and the army of cult members that invaded her home. After all, she had also been elevated to prestigious position of apostle. But it soon became apparent that Credonia resented the strictures normally associated with being a visitor. She wanted to run things in the Kibwetere home. According to her, the home (which had now become the headquarters of a flourishing cult movement) had to be managed in accordance with specific instructions communicated to her by the Virgin Mary.

Kibwetere was instructed to take his children out of school because it was no good attending earthly schools; that much the Virgin had revealed to Credonia. The earthly teachers were too corrupt and too worldly. One only needed to cast a casual glance at the syllabus to discover that it prepared pupils for a position in Satan's ranks. The curriculum encouraged pupils to learn mathematics, English, history, geography and other such arcane worldly topics, completely unmeritorious when, sooner or later, they had to appear before their Creator on judgement day. The children were better off being prepared for salvation, which was coming soon. Credonia instructed Kibwetere to start a boarding school for his own children and those of other cult members where the syllabus would prepare them for the end of time. Her will was done.

Amidst much fanfare, spiced by speeches from important local political luminaries, who made it a point never to miss out on ceremonies generous in free eats and drinks, the cult officially opened Ishayuriiro rya Maria Primary School on their hilltop compound. To tongues uninitiated in the languages of western Uganda this translates roughly as Rescue Place for the Virgin Mary Primary School[29]. At this school prayer was an important ritual that took place before transacting any other school business. Pupils lined up in neat columns at seven o'clock and one of the apostles led them in prayer. Naturally, reciting "Holy Mary" was standard practice.

In the cult school, teaching was mainly focused on the Ten Commandments and constant reminders about the importance of obedience to one's teachers and parents. It was hammered into the children's heads that they must at all times show total and undivided loyalty to cult leaders. They were told that the cult leaders had been chosen by God to guide them away from the dangers of AIDS and many other deadly punishments that awaited non-believers in a not too distant future.

Austerity was the watchword in the boarding school since it was perceived to be necessary to veer young minds away from idleness and frivolity. Pupils slept on the bare cement floor with no blankets to shield them from the cold night. And the refectory table was equally mean. A thin maize porridge was served for lunch and pupils were required to spend the hot afternoon toiling in the cult's large fields of maize, bananas and beans. Other pupils were deployed to collect firewood or fetch water from a well in the valley below. Little surprise then that most of the pupils suffered from malnutrition and malaria, and respiratory diseases were also a constant menace.

Ugandan boarding schools (modelled along a prison system, as some are apt to state) are not famous for their comfort, but the conditions in the cult school were beyond the usual accepted horrors of internment in the guise of getting pupils literate and numerate. In 1998, after a visit from an official of the Department of Education, the school was forced to close, the closure notice citing "engaging in acts that violated the Constitution of the Republic of Uganda, the local Government Act and the Public Health regulations" as reasons for this unusual step. Besides, said this official, a thoroughly decent man, we do not go to school for the sole purpose of being prepared for the apocryphal end of the world.

Credonia, who once dressed in the sexiest mini-skirts while working the streets was now condemning anybody in the Kibwetere compound who dared to dress in any clothes other than long flowing robes, which were the recommended cult uniforms. She claimed the Virgin Mary had given her samples of the sort of clothes to be worn by followers of the ***Movement for Restoration of the Ten Commandments of God***. At the height of her haughtiness she bundled up Theresa Kibwetere's clothes and burnt them[30]. A witness to this incident, which happened while Theresa was away, remembers especially the look in Credonia's eyes. "She stared at the flames like one possessed by Chwezi spirits. When the clothes had completely burnt and were a heap of black ashes, she burst out in hysterical laughter that lasted for at least five minutes. At first we thought she had gone crazy."

As for Theresa, she was distraught at the loss of her expensive dresses. In desperation, she tried to discuss the matter with her husband and persuade him to expel Credonia from their home. Instead Joseph Kibwetere was offended by his wife's ingratitude and couldn't understand how she could be so unreasonable. He demanded his wife tell him what one gained by hanging on to the material things of this world? Patiently, he explained to her that standard cult uniform worn by followers was definitely far more beautiful than wrapping oneself in garments made by earthly tailors. In effect Kibwetere was ordering his wife to forget completely the luxury of wearing the flashy and beautiful designs paraded in the streets of Uganda by the rich and glamorous ladies. Besides, Kibwetere told Theresa, as the wife of the leader of the ***Movement for the Restoration of the Ten Commandments of God***, she had to be exemplary.

Theresa was not impressed. She continued mourning the loss of her dresses and her distrust of and distaste for Credonia Mwerinde and her sister Ursula Komuhangi deepened. These two had conspired with her husband to make life a living hell for her. And as time went on she began viewing them all as a group of impostors whose visions were nothing but lies and hallucinations.

One particular incident, sometime after the burning of her clothes, bothered her and set her to rethink whether it was really worthwhile to remain associated with this pack of newfangled visionaries. It came in the form of a strange request that Joseph Kibwetere made to some of his loyal followers. He instructed them to buy a coffin, which they proceeded to fill with stones. Once finished they hurried off to collect his wife "to bury her husband"[31] . But Theresa insisted on opening the coffin, a request firmly denied. Her suspicions aroused, she alerted police. There was disbelief when police officers forced the coffin open only to find rocks. The idea behind this strange ploy was to have the faithful believe that the "prophet" had died. According to the plan, Kibwetere would resurrect three days later, just like Jesus Christ. One ex-cult follower said, "If he had succeeded in this ruse he would probably have declared himself Jesus Christ." Theresa was not amused. She declined to play along and began exploring ways of getting the group out of her home.

A few years after Kibwetere failed miserably to demonstrate his immortality, another cult leader would emerge on the Uganda scene with similar claims. This was the self-proclaimed prophetess, Nabaasa Gwajwa, whose youthfulness was equated with "the truth, the whole truth, and nothing but the truth." She claimed to have undergone a painful death sometime in 1996, resurrecting four days later vested with miraculous qualities. Nabaasa's religious group is yet another striking example of where traditional African belief coexists with Christian practice. The prophetess combines Bible teaching with Chwezi spiritual practices. Judging by the crowds that follow every single footstep the prophetess makes, it is evident that her immortality is taken seriously. Villagers in this remote area of western Uganda where Nabaasa Gwajwa conducted her healing crusades testified as to how the prophetess had cured their sick children or ailing relatives.

Particular praise was showered upon her for success in healing the mentally ill. There was a story doing the rounds of the spectacular healing of a schizophrenic niece of a high-ranking military man. Even supposedly enlightened folk who didn't believe her story outright gave her the benefit of the doubt. The president, himself a native of the region, most probably heard about these stories while vacationing at his ranch in Rwakitura, not far off from Nabaasa's base. Impressed and intrigued by the prophetess' claim, Yoweri Museveni organised a meeting with Nabaasa. It was on the basis of this meeting that the president of the Republic of Uganda appointed a special commission to investigate the miraculous deeds of this young woman who had so impressed him[32].

As a symbol of his spiritual leadership and authority within the movement, Kibwetere chose to adhere to a dress code befitting a devout spiritual leader. He discarded the earthly looking khaki safari suits, replacing them with something more appropriate for the prince of the church. With his background as a lay teacher in the Catholic Church it is not surprising that the choice fell on a cassock. And not any cassock would do. Apparently, as head of a flock of believers, he saw no difference between himself and a bishop of the mainstream Christian church. He picked a purple cassock with a black sash around the waist, and a golden ring on his finger crowned his new ecclesiastical look. It is apparent, therefore, that replacing the safari suit for the cassock was not in any way an exercise in humility and austerity; it was to equate and ally him with powerful spiritual leaders of the Catholic Church.

There was also a dress code for the followers which, as we have already observed, Credonia Mwerinde tried to enforce on Theresa Kibwetere. The cult preached that followers were heavenly brides and had to dress accordingly. And they could choose their robes from three colours—white, black and green. After undergoing spiritual rebirth, Credonia and the other female apostles swathed themselves in white floor-length dresses and white veils. If you happened to bump into these female apostles you would be forgiven for thinking they belonged to some bona fide Catholic religious order. With their white habits fluttering about in the dusty wind they looked like a group of conservative Catholic nuns. But these women were ultra conservative in their dress code, scoffing at their mainstream post-modern counterparts who had discarded the austere habit, a symbol of their marriage to Christ, in preference for dresses that went a less than decent length above the knees[33].

Kataribabo and two other errant Catholic priests in cult service wore black suits with white Roman collars to distinguish them from the laity. Although excommunicated the three still considered themselves as Catholic priests and were in total agreement with Catholic Church pronouncements on the issue of dress code for the priesthood. According to Canon 284 of Canon Law a cleric of the Church should dress in "suitable clerical clothing, according to the norms issued by the Episcopal Conference and according to legitimate local customs." Therefore, these three priests sought to show proudly to all and sundry that they had dedicated their lives to Christ and evidence was to be seen in their wearing of the Roman collar, which is a hallmark of a priest in Uganda and in much of the Christian world.

People who had contributed substantial amounts of money or property to the movement upon entry wore green garments. And the ordinary peasantry, the hoi polloi, with little to give at enrolment, had to do with black flowing robes. Thus, altruism or any pretence to it played little or no part in the doctrine of the group. And nobody, male or female, adult or child was permitted to wear any undergarments for reasons that had to do with hygiene, or so they were told. No other colours except the official ones were tolerated either. And could a mini skirt in the approved colours be acceptable? Over the cult leaders' dead bodies! Females had to wear dresses that completely covered that sexually provocative part of their anatomy—the thigh. Exposure of thighs would distract male worshippers from prayer, it was argued. It would cause men to stumble from pursuit of a greater spiritual fulfilment by wallowing in libidinous evil thoughts that led to the big fall-out between man and God in the Garden of Eden. Donning robes that swept the ground ensured that female members of the cult were in no position to cause males to stumble in their faith, so went cult philosophy.

Their leaders told the cultists that by having chosen to leave their families and follow the ***Movement for the Restoration of the Ten Commandments of God***, they had been completely absolved of their sins. And, as a people without sin, they had to have physical characteristics that distanced them from sinners, anarchists, rebels and the corrupt—groups that were well represented in Uganda society. And for those who might have found these arguments a bit too mundane, there was a more practical and compelling consideration.

It was part of cult preaching that when the last trumpet sounds, pronouncing the end of sinful Mother Earth, angels would have their work of ferrying off the true believers made easy. The faithful would stand out distinctly in their white, black or green robes. And as to the odd man in purple, well, he was part of the heavenly entourage and the flock needn't worry about him missing the boat. The dress code was strictly adhered to at all time on cult compound. For those who ever dared to violate or challenge the dress code, expulsion awaited.

In 1991 the cult relocated its activities to Kanungu after Theresa and her children finally marshalled enough courage to kick the movement out of their Ruguma home[34]. On the surface, the transfer of the cult headquarters to a place where Credonia had been ridiculed and despised looks surprising. However, this was the only practicable and logical course open to the cult. As it was, Credonia had just succeeded in converting her father, Paul Kashaku, after much cajoling and threats of damnation if he persisted in rejecting his daughter's message of salvation.

Initially, Credonia's father had scoffed at her apparition claims. Paul Kashaku even warned the people of Kanungu not to follow his crazy daughter. He felt he had a responsibility as their catechist to steer them away from satanic organisations—just like the one led by his daughter. Clearly, here was a man who could stand against his own flesh and blood when it came to defending the fundamental teachings of the Roman Catholic Church.

But Credonia eventually won him over to her movement. She confronted him with evidence of ordained Catholic priests who believed in and proclaimed the messages she had received from the Madonna and queried the logic of a spiritually lowly catechist rejecting what his betters had already discerned as divine truth. Unable to counter this logic her father quit the Catholic Church and his position as a catechist, choosing instead to direct his energies serving the cause of his daughter's spiritual movement.

When he became a follower of the movement, no other member of the cult could match Paul Kashaku in the fervency of his belief in

Credonia's visions and messages. Just as the cult was groping about in darkness wondering where to establish their earthly headquarters Credonia's father came to their rescue. He owned a large tract of land in Kanungu that he willingly turned over to the cult. And it was theirs at no cost. What magnanimity! For his act of charity Kashaku was rewarded with a special appointment. It was communicated to him that the selfless gesture of donating land had pleased Jesus Christ extremely and for that he had earned his place among the disciples.

Because of his donation and the fact that he was the father of two seers, Credonia and Ursula, he enjoyed a special status that was only superseded by that of Credonia Mwerinde. Clear testimony of this fact was evident when a *New Vision* journalist visited the cult compound in Kanungu a year before it was destroyed. When asked about the origins of the spiritual movement, cultists informed the journalist that it had all started with this former village catechist. Kashaku is reputed to have had apparitions from the Virgin Mary and Jesus Christ, just like the rest of the cult leadership, with instructions to go out into the world and preach a new message of salvation before the soon approaching end of the world. Even the seemingly immortal die and then the bereaved try to build a powerful myth of invincibility around the expired soul. This is just what happened to the simple catechist of Kanungu, Paul Kashaku. When he died a Church was built around his burial place and an altar erected right above his grave[35].

On this donated patch of prime fertile land, Kibwetere and his cult built their headquarters. Besides the church, there were two dormitories—one for females and children and the other for males. Save for the lowing of about fifty cows imported from Europe (no mean feat, owning such an impressive herd in a hostile Ugandan climate), an aura of eerie silence ruled the place. Cultists scurried from farm to church or to the numerous holy shrines scattered around the compound in total silence. A policy of not using the spoken word to communicate was strictly enforced. Necessary, they said, to maintain discipline and to prevent members from living like cat and dog. Most importantly, however, the code of silence protected against breaking the Eighth Commandment.

Sign language was taught to aid day-to-day communication. The only time cultists had the opportunity to use their vocal cords while on the cult compound was during prayer in church or at the obligatory Saturday penance before one of the cult priests. Of course, apostles and the ones who had donated generously to cult coffers were exempted from this stringent rule that literally muzzled the mouths of cultists.

Donating unreservedly was the kind of gesture expected of an ardent follower. According to cult teachings, followers were urged to act just like Jesus Christ's disciples, who left all material things in their possession and decided to follow Christ. But unlike Jesus and his disciples, cult followers were requested to sell their property and turn over the cash to the cult leadership.

Another parallel that the cult gave as an example to encourage followers to hand over property was the story of Abraham. It was preached that Abraham was called by God and instructed to leave his homeland and go to a place that would be shown to him. In this journey to the Promised Land of Canaan he moved with all his property. Therefore, the cult leadership preached, followers who had failed to sell their property could bring it along to the cult compound in Kanungu.

Once such material goods entered the cult compound, however, they became the sole property of the cult and were quickly disposed off to the highest bidder. Followers were told that the money was needed to initiate and complete special projects that had been chosen carefully by the Virgin Mary or Jesus Christ.

One such worthy project was the construction of special houses referred to as "the arks". These would serve as safe havens for thousands of followers during the three days of darkness—a central theme in cult teaching. This and other cult doctrines were supposedly revealed as divine truths to Credonia Mwerinde, Joseph Kibwetere, Father Dominic Kataribabo and numerous other cult leaders, the so-called twelve disciples.

Chapter 5
The Ten Commandments

If you do not obey faithfully all God's teachings that are written in this book and if you do not honour the wonderful and awesome name of the Lord your God, he will send on you and on your descendants incurable diseases and horrible epidemics that can never be stopped. Deuteronomy 28:58-59

Most of the world's religions have writings considered sacred by the faithful. Such writings serve as a blueprint in pursuance of higher spiritual goals. And the ***Movement for the Restoration of the Ten Commandments of God*** was no exception. Its most sacred book was called *"A timely message from heaven: the end of the present times"*. The ex-Catholic priest, Dominic Kataribabo, was the intellectual force behind its writing. This book documented all the apparitions that apostles and seers of the movement supposedly received from the Virgin Mary and Jesus Christ. The movement's spiritual book mainly conveys messages of righteous living with a typically Ugandan flavour, and highlights are described below.

On 14th June1989 a message to restore the Ten Commandments of the Lord was revealed to Credonia Mwerinde. It was a message that she had to take to the entire world without discriminating on basis of race, religious denomination or gender, for the Virgin Mary had stated, "*All who live are my children.*" And to add weight to the importance of conveying the message without excluding anybody, Jesus Christ added his voice thus, "*I died on the cross for all people irrespective of their religious denomination. Be it that you are Christian, Muslim or even pagan, I shed my blood for you.*" Credonia was ordered to inform the world that the Madonna and her son had been compelled to return to this world because of their great love for the human race. They wanted to save our part of the universe from eternal damnation.

The Ten Commandments that the Lord had handed down to Moses on Mount Sinai were the key that unlocked the door of eternal happiness. However, instead of showing allegiance to the Lord God, who created all that lives and has ever lived, men had deserted those commandments, choosing to live instead according to human values riddled with sin and corruption, preferring to serve Satan, the prince of darkness. It was a state of affairs totally unacceptable to God and because of this, the Lord had written off mankind as unworthy to share in the inheritance of eternal salvation. Now destruction awaited them.

Credonia was supposedly lifted to heaven where an aggrieved heavenly father spoke to the Madonna thus, "*The people of this generation are unworthy of being called my children. One by one I will destroy them as punishment for their disobedience*." But the Madonna interceded on behalf of sinful mankind. On her knees she begged and pleaded with the Lord, "*My Lord and God, before you subject them to total destruction permit me to travel to the world and show myself to them. Perhaps by seeing me and hearing about their transgressions mankind might repent and return to observance of the Ten Commandments*." The Lord God did not think the Madonna stood a chance of turning mankind away from the path of sin—for sin appeared to be this world's natural way.

Then the Lord reminded the Virgin Mary about Christ's first coming to Earth and the brutal manner in which he had been mistreated. Jesus Christ had shown mankind what was required to achieve eternal salvation. He had performed numerous miraculous deeds, which included healing the sick, restoring sight to the blind and hearing to the deaf. But corrupt mankind under the stewardship of Satan had not listened to him. Instead the children of darkness had chosen to crucify the Son of God on the cross. "*For so corrupt a people, I will give them what they deserve*," said the Lord God to Mary in the presence of Credonia.

Then the Virgin Mary prostrated herself before the throne of the Lord God pleading, "*My Lord and my God, allow me to go to them. Maybe out of one thousand, I will manage to save one or two souls*." But the Lord was not willing to let the Virgin Mary return to a world whose foolish and unreasonable inhabitants might subject her to the same fate that they had dealt her son. Then Jesus

Christ supported his mother saying, "*Please father, let me go down with her. If we cannot save them then my blood would have been shed in vain.*"

But the Lord God remained unmoved. Jesus then suggested that the Lord God allow him and Mary to speak to mankind through other people. It was an idea that the Lord God found favourable. He wanted the Virgin Mary and Jesus Christ to impress upon mankind that He was particularly offended and distressed at the rampant violation of the commandment that forbade adultery. They were instructed to inform mankind that as a show of his displeasure at the wanton fornication and utter lewdness that characterised life on earth, the Lord God had decided to release a terrible punishment for violation of the laws against adultery. That punishment was the well-known disease AIDS. Unless mankind repented and rejected their practice of fornicating like dogs on heat there would be no cure for AIDS. To those who would listen to the Lord God's plea to refrain from adultery, even if suffering from an advanced stage of the disease, an instant cure would be provided.

For those who refused to repent their sins and continued to break the Ten Commandments, the Lord God would ensure that punishment for their transgressions began right away. And there were even more terrible chastisements that waited in the everlasting sulphurous fire of hell, where the fornicators would groan and grind their teeth in indescribable pain. The Lord God would not show them any mercy, for they had squandered golden opportunities to return to his flock.

However, a way was being opened for sinful mankind to win the favour of the Lord God once again. On this road to reconciliation certain things were critical, according to the truth revealed to Credonia Mwerinde. Top of the list was total and unconditional rejection of envy—a principal tool that Satan employed in bringing about discord in human relationships, hence paving way for breaking the Ten Commandments. Envy leads to selfishness and sense of pride, the Lord revealed to Credonia. It is also the source of disagreements, fraud, hypocrisy and anger. Envy creates rudeness, hatred and enmity. Instead of these vices humanity should cultivate faith, hope, charity and forgiveness. Of all virtues that the Lord God desires in mankind none surpasses strict adherence to the observation of the Ten Commandments.

According to the spiritual movement's book *"A timely message from heaven: the end of the present times"* the Virgin Mary and Jesus Christ continued instructing Credonia on numerous occasions. Credonia was ordered to urge God's children to cleanse their hearts and prepare themselves for salvation. Preparing oneself for salvation entails receiving all sacraments with one's heart and soul. The Madonna and her son reminded the Lord God's children that sacraments are the oils greasing the wheel of prayer. In order to pray meaningfully those seeking salvation must read the psalms and other writings that have been inspired by the Lord God.

Meaningful prayer is best done in Church, in the presence of other believers. Therefore, it is the divine desire that those who have turned their backs on the Church must return. Congregating must be driven purely by spiritual motives and in no instance should this be for worldly gains. And woe shall befall those who go to church for reasons of seeking out their debtors. The church is God's house and not a market place. Nor is it a chatting shop, as some people like to believe. These chatterboxes say, "Well, wouldn't it be nice to go to church and confront my debtors." But God's house is not a trading house. Only a wholesome and sincere desire to congregate in order to bring praise and glory to the name of the living God would be acknowledged on judgement day.

Of those that are tempted to go to the Lord's house for reasons other than this, eternal damnation awaits. In this category are those people that view churchgoing as an opportunity to discuss sinister motives with their comrades-in-arms in the business of violating the Ten Commandments. Of particular concern to the Madonna are the murderers who turn up in churches, not for prayer but for plotting strategy on how best to eliminate their next victim.

According to Credonia's account, the Virgin Mary and Jesus Christ told her to pass on the following message to the people of this world. Before going to church it is important that you go through a process of self-reflection and find out if you have broken any of the Ten Commandments. Punctuality in church is of utmost importance for reasons of receiving the sacrament of penance. Priests have the authority to dispense forgiveness only at the very beginning of mass and for this reason believers are urged to be punctual for mass. Those who oversleep, choosing to walk into church in the middle of mass, are therefore unlikely to receive forgiveness for their sins.

And church going has its obligations, so said the Madonna to Credonia. The laity must help the church leadership unreservedly when it comes to supporting church projects financially. Many complain that church dues are prohibitive, and for this reason choose to desert the church. But surely, asked the Virgin Mary, how is it possible that the very ones feigning poverty are more than willing to bequeath large sums of money to witchdoctors for services dedicated to Satan? And aren't these very people prepared to sacrifice any number of goats, sheep and cows just because the witchdoctors order them to? If they can do this of their own free will, then their arguments that churches ask for too much money from members are as hollow as the sound of an empty tin.

The Lord God would like to see his children contributing more to his causes than continuing to fill Satan's coffers. If a church roof is leaking and leaders request monetary contributions, Christians should not say, "We are sick and tired of being asked to donate money. Instead of contributing this money to the Church we would rather use it in the pub." Church leaders are not oblivious to the general state of poverty of their congregations and it is for this reason that they only ask for a pittance.

The laity spends a generous amount of their income on alcohol and debauchery. It is this kind of irresponsible drinking that turns people into Satan's slaves. To those tempted to drink alcohol this is a warning from Jesus Christ: "*A drunkard breaks all the Ten Commandments of God in a twinkle of an eye*." And Jesus went on to explain to Credonia how the drunkard goes about violating every conceivable law of the Lord.

Early in the morning the drunkard awakes to be greeted by a hangover. Disoriented in time and space, he is not sure if he had had a decent meal the previous day or during the entire week. In panic he rummages through his pockets and to his consternation, retrieves an impressive wad of crispy notes. "How the dickens did so much money find its way into my pockets?" he inquires. In truth, the barmaid-cum-prostitute had stolen the money the previous evening from a rich client, and in turn the drunkard had stolen it from the prostitute during their brief sex encounter. There, the Seventh Commandment is flouted.

Then comes a flood of accusations from angry village mates. "Last night, while in the bar, you falsely accused us of bewitching our neighbour's cows." At a total loss about the goings on of the previous night, the drunkard swears in the name of the living Lord and denies all the charges. With this denial the drunkard breaks the Eighth Commandment.

Just when he is about to proceed to a restaurant to stuff his mouth full with chunks of roast goat, he is surrounded by a crowd accusing him of having been in company of a rowdy group of drunks that had raped and killed a schoolgirl the previous evening. Stunned, he vigorously but vainly tries to deny the truth. Thus, his actions have succeeded in shattering two commandments in one go; thus are the Fifth and Sixth Commandments thrown to the wind.

And to you, the evil sorcerers, devious architects of evil, the Lord God will punish you without mercy if you remain belligerent in pursuit of your malign dark arts and refuse to repent and recognise his greatness and undying love. Repent now, for the Lord God wants you to burn your amulets and talismans and return to his fold. Do not be deceived by the false sense of security that you derive from your satanic fetishes. The Lord is waiting for your repentance now. On judgement day the very fetishes that they trusted will confront all those sorcerers who had denied the Lord their God. Then the Lord God will speak thus, "*You trusted Satan with all his fetishes and even led others astray. Here, take all your amulets and talismans and off you go to hell to entertain your master Satan with wailing and gnashing of your teeth.*" The Virgin Mary, our loving mother, appeals to all you witchdoctors and all the sinful to repent and detach yourselves from the grip of Satan. The Virgin Mary and Jesus Christ emphasised to Credonia Mwerinde that there was just enough time for all the sinful to repent, and that time was now.

Satan has taken over the people of God and continues to conquer more territory with each passing day, said Jesus Christ and his mother. The people of this generation complain, "Why did the Lord abandon us to Satan and his treacherous vices?" Surely the Lord your God promised you inheritance in heaven only if you denounced your evil ways and turned to him through obeying the Ten Commandments. In his treacherous way Satan usurped the Ten Commandments replacing them with his own laws, which are the exact opposites of God's commandments. As for those of you who accept to live by satanic laws, eternal damnation awaits. But the good news is: Satan cannot control those who believe in the Lord God.

God created man and endowed him with three parts. There is the physical body that takes charge of such things like procreation, and which has to be nurtured with food and water. It is the body that man deploys to cultivate his fields of maize, beans or bananas. Humans also have a second part—the soul. It is the soul that yearns and hungers for the divine. And it is this same soul that guides mankind in observing the Ten Commandments. When a person dies, it is this part that goes to heaven. Finally, humans also have an evil force within. This evil force can only be developed with the help of Satan, and it is this force within mankind that establishes contact with Lu cifer. However, a well-developed soul overwhelms and vanquishes this evil force and causes it to shrivel and die. Thus concludes the Virgin Mary, "*In this way, you people of this generation are composed of three parts*."

The Madonna and her son had returned to this world in order to destroy that evil third part within mankind. This they would do by working through the chosen apostles of the ***Movement for Restoration of the Ten Commandments of God***. These apostles had been instructed to organise courses in which God's children would learn how to kill the evil force within their beings. God intended that humanity should only have two parts—body and soul. Material things and money belong to the evil force. The children of God were therefore urged to give these up. As for those consorting with Satan, a triple six sign has been marked on their right arm or forehead.

Satan's children, with their triple six sign, freely indulge in eating, drinking and committing adultery. Satan encourages them to engage in unnatural sexual unions. It was for this very reason that the Lord God brought his wrath to bear upon Sodom and Gomorrah. In some countries men are already marrying fellow men and women are doing likewise. All these are signs that Satan has now been released and is freely roaming the length and breadth of the earth in search of recruits for his devilish army. He infiltrates churches where he encourages worshippers to drum and shout ecstatically all in the name of prayer[36].

At such gatherings Satan even makes outlandish and extravagant claims that he is Christ and promises all sorts of miraculous deeds, like bringing the dead back to life. But it is a relatively easy matter for seers to identify the true Christ. The real Christ has scars in his hands whereas Satan claiming to be Christ usually appears as a cross without the Lord's image.

The cheeky Satan also appears to many people in the guise of the Virgin Mary. The twelve anointed apostles have been given the knowledge to make the distinction between a false and real Madonna. The false Madonna appears wearing mini-dresses and has no halo, heavenly light or crown. In the event of an apparition it is impossible for the sinner to make this distinction.

Lots of other smaller devils roam the countryside masquerading as angels. But in reality these are Chwezi spirits with their in-depth understanding of the church's prayers. They mastered these prayers during their brief stay in heaven before the rebellion that led to their expulsion. Once they possess a person, they order him to buy a Bible or another religious book depending on their faith. Then the evil spirits proceed to teach the person false doctrine. If given an opportunity to enter and posses their victim they cause drowsiness and boredom, especially when the person tries to perform sacred rites like prayer. Therefore, the Madonna and her son instruct the apostles to go out and exorcise these evil spirits in order to set God's children free.

Credonia Mwerinde was further instructed by the Madonna and her son to impress on everyone the urgency of restoring the Ten Commandments. And the laws of the Lord should not be observed partially; all the Ten Commandments must be strictly observed. Mankind needn't wait for a vision of the Virgin Mary or Jesus Christ before realising the importance of returning to the Ten Commandments. Time is running out and repentance must happen now, the Virgin Mary stressed to Credonia. Disobedience of the Commandments in these last days would have serious and far-reaching repercussions. Then Credonia was given examples of what lay in store for those that persisted in disobedience.

The Lord God will ensure that the sinner never succeeds in any money-generating enterprise. And should the sinner hold high-office, he will not be able to execute his duties as required of him. Married couples will have terrible misunderstandings and daily quarrels will replace the normal matrimonial harmony. Tired of same sex unions, sinners will resort to bestiality in search of sexual gratification. Men will seek lionesses and leopards. Women will fight for mountain gorillas and baboons. And how blinded and consumed they will be in pursuit of worldly success and worthless conquest! For example, the one with a wheelbarrow will desire a bicycle. And the owner of a bicycle will hunger for a motorcycle. The motorcyclist will crave for a car. Upon owning the car, the long sought after happiness will remain elusive. Mankind will be blinded by desire to achieve and possess more. But all this longing and achievements will not guarantee peace of mind. Instead, there will be more misery, hatred and jealousy, which will culminate in the unrepentant sinners finding themselves in eternal hellfire.

Joseph Kibwetere's first encounter with Jesus Christ and the Blessed Virgin Mary is supposed to have taken place on 25th April 1984. He was requested to denounce sin and prepare himself for the gigantic and difficult task of leading God's children back to strict observance of the Ten Commandments. Jesus Christ spoke to him thus, "*Joseph Kibwetere, time is ripe for you to go out and gather the Lord's rich harvest lest all is lost. You have been specially anointed to teach my people about ways of restoring the Ten Commandments.*" Observance of the Ten Commandments is the all-important yardstick that the Lord God will use to save or condemn the people of this generation. Then Jesus Christ and his mother handed him the Ten Commandments and told him the significance of each of the laws.

"*I am the Lord your God who brought you out of Egypt, where you were slaves. Worship no god but me. Do not make for yourselves images or anything in heaven or on earth or in the water under the earth. Do not bow down to any idol or worship it, because I am the Lord your God and I tolerate no rivals. I bring punishment on those who hate me and on their descendants down to the third and fourth generation. But I show my love to thousands of generations of those who love me and obey my laws.*" This is the first commandment of the Almighty God to his children (Exodus 20:2-6). The Lord God says that the first commandment is a call to his children to worship, obey and love him above all other things. Therefore, strict observance of the first commandment means you shall not give allegiance, completely or partially, to Satan, sorcerers and wizards. Ancestor worship is strictly forbidden.

"*Do not use my name for evil purposes, for I, the Lord your God, will punish anyone who misuses my name.*" That is the second commandment (Exodus 20:7). It forbids bringing dishonour to the name of God. For the name of God is great and feared. God's name is worshipped in heaven and on earth. Woe to all those who appear in courts, take an oath with their hands on the Bible, and yet proceed to give false testimony. And woe shall befall the blasphemous that profane the name of our Lord. For all these are in contravention of the Second Commandment.

"*Observe the Sabbath and keep it holy. You have six days in which to do your work, but the seventh day is a day of rest dedicated to me. On that day no one is to work—neither you, your children, your slaves, your animals, nor the foreigners who live in your country. In six days I, the Lord, made the earth, the sky, the sea, and everything in them, but on the seventh day I rested. That is why I, the Lord, blessed the Sabbath and made it holy.* " This is the Third Commandment (Exodus 20:8-11). The Sabbath falls on Sunday, a day that ought to be dedicated to the Lord God. He honoured it by raising his son from the dead. The Holy

Spirit, the helper, was also sent to the world on Sunday. Therefore, Sunday is of special significance to the Lord God, and everybody must get on their knees and praise the Almighty on this holy day.

Reserve Sunday for strict prayer and deep contemplation. All the Lord's children are forbidden to do any work that might bring sweat to the brow. There should be no cooking on this holy day. The only activities that are tolerated on Sunday are visiting the sick or ministering to non-practising Christians in an effort to win them back to the Lord. Also tolerated are the activities of the apostles of the ***Movement for the Restoration of the Ten Commandments of God*** involving spreading the divinely revealed message to God's children. Anything undertaken on Sunday that does not fall within these three categories is violation of the Third Commandment.

Alas, children of this generation! You have chosen Sunday as an occasion to profane the Lord's commands. Much of the drinking and most abortions are now scheduled for Sunday. Instead of worshipping and praising the Lord's name, lots of people decide to visit Chwezi sorcerers who insist that their prophecies can only be told on Sundays. It is also on Sunday that immoral relationships come to total fruition. Sunday should be returned to the Lord. That is what fulfilment of the Third Commandment demands.

The Fourth Commandment (Exodus 20:12) states, "*Respect your father and your mother, so that you may live a long time in the land that I am giving you.*" It obliges us to show respect and honour to our parents, civic and religious leaders. We must, therefore, obey them with all our soul and show unquestioning willingness to assist them in all activities they assign to us. It goes without saying that children who shun their responsibilities and spend much of their time drinking are violating the Fourth Commandment. Accordingly, parents are charged with ensuring that their children learn and obey the Ten Commandments. Parents should ensure that their children are trained in skills that bring honour and praise to the Lord's name.

The Fifth Commandment (Exodus 20:13) says, "*Do not commit murder.*" Implicitly, this commandment forbids us to wish others ill. For this can kill their souls. We are also forbidden to use medicines that might promote abortion. Birth control pills are also forbidden.

Euthanasia is not allowed. Drinking alcohol and smoking of tobacco are strictly forbidden[37]. Alcohol and tobacco cause fatal disease. The Fifth Command also forbids careless driving. A careless driver might cause the death of passengers[38]. Carelessness in driving means being on the road with a car in a dangerous mechanical condition or driving under influence of alcohol or drugs. In order to be in a good position to obey the Fifth Commandment, motorists are urged to be conversant with the Highway Code.

"*Do not commit adultery.*" That is the Sixth Commandment (Exodus 20:14). And this is closely related to the Ninth Commandment (Exodus 20:17), "*Do not desire another man's wife.*" Adultery can take many forms. The first form of it is known as "active participation in adulterous acts". Under this category, one may engage in adulterous acts either alone or with one or more partners. The partner may be of the same or different sex. The second form of adultery is "adulterous talk". This includes talking or singing obscenities. Reading letters or books containing adulterous words falls under this category. Also forbidden is listening to immoral words that arouse sinful carnal desires. These commandments also forbid watching pornographic films. One might feel an urge to engage in an adulterous act or to fornicate, but due to some reason fail to execute it. The very act of desiring such a sinful act is a grave violation of the Commandments. And for that, the Lord God will punish you. Also forbidden under these Commandments, but especially the Sixth, are laziness, loitering and dancing styles with obscene, immoral movements.

"*Do not steal.*" That is the Seventh Commandment (Exodus 20:15). And it is closely related to the Tenth (Exodus 20:17), which states, "*Do not desire another man's house; his slaves, his cattle, his donkeys, or anything that he owns.*" Jesus and the Madonna explained to Kibwetere the four different categories of stealing. The first category is the common thief with a habit of pinching what belongs to others. The second group consists of children who steal from parents, just because they want to have more. Traders who overcharge for their goods or services are grouped separately into a third category. The fourth group consists of those persons who ask for payment for tasks they never performed. All these groups are in violation of God's Commandments and will be punished accordingly. If you fall into any of these categories and wish to be reconciled with observance of the Seventh Commandment then you are obliged to return all stolen property to its rightful owners.

The Eighth Commandment (Exodus 20:16) states, "*Do not accuse anyone falsely.*" This Commandment also forbids us telling lies. Making jokes at the expense of others is also forbidden under this Commandment. It also warns us against talking ill of our family, friends or neighbours. When someone entrusts you with a secret and you break the promise, it is the Eighth Commandment that you are breaking. After revealing the Commandments, Jesus and the Madonna once again instructed Kibwetere, "*Go and reveal all the Ten Commandments to God's children. Whoever shall listen to you and repent will share the inheritance of heaven. Those persisting in their evil ways, violating the Ten Commandments, the Lord God will banish in hellfire.*"

Another prominent cult leader that claimed to have had apparitions was the Reverend Father Dominic Kataribabo. It was sometime in the late evening of 19th December 1990 when the priest, sitting alone at dinner in his Rugazi residence, heard a soft knock on his door. At the same time he noticed an aura of holiness engulfing the room. It was as if thick but invisible clouds had filled the room. Being a trained and pious priest, he had immediately discerned that he stood in the presence of holiness. Quickly, but making sure to remain composed, he had removed his shoes and crawled on his knees as he went to answer the door. That is the account that Father Dominic Kataribabo gave of his first encounter with Jesus the Messiah. What followed was a pleasant and congenial conversation between the two.

Christ had ordered Kataribabo to go and preach to the children of this generation about the Sacrament of Penance. It is through receipt of this Sacrament that Christ dispenses forgiveness to those for whom he died on the cross. Of late, however, disturbing developments in the manner that priests dispense this Sacrament had forced Jesus Christ to stop pardoning the children of this generation.

In the name of modernity and renewal, many priests were lending general absolution. This was unacceptable, stressed Jesus. Every individual sinner should be made to face and account for his or her own sins. Blanket amnesties, which are extended to a congregation without taking into account the uniqueness of individual sin, are therefore not binding either on earth or heaven.

Jesus likened such general absolutions to a judge who decides to give the same sentence to one hundred people brought before him without taking into account the gravity of their crimes. If mortal man and his corrupt justice system do not operate this way then why should the Lord use a standard far short of a human yardstick? Besides, because there was no individual accountability, people felt free to continue committing the very same sins.

Jesus reportedly told Kataribabo that for survival of this generation it was imperative to restore the Sacrament of Penance to its proper and original state. Sinners must go individually to their priests and in the quiet and safety of a confession booth reveal their sins. No detail should be omitted. Both small and big violations of the Commandments had to be confessed. Because the sinner was required to reveal actions and thoughts in violation of God's Commandments nobody would be willing to go through the agony of recounting the same sins time and again before a priest. Therefore, the only course open to such a person was to put an end to committing those particular sins. It is then clear that through individual confession the feeling of shame would reduce the number of sinners, and the observance of God's Ten Commandments would be restored in full glory.

Outside the main message on the Sacrament of Penance, Jesus Christ purportedly entrusted Father Dominic Kataribabo with another message for the priests. This is what Christ had to say to church ministers: "*All of you who are anointed have the responsibility of celebrating the Eucharist, administering Sacraments and proclaiming God's Good News.*" Therefore, priests must not spend time condemning the activities of the ***Movement for the Restoration of the Ten Commandments of God***, for the divine message had been revealed to a chosen few. If they are indeed righteous priests they should be able to feel the Spirit of God that is active in these last days of the world.

A cursory look at the Scriptures and attention to what was happening on earth was evidence enough to show that what the prophets predicted thousands of years ago was already happening. It was the Spirit that spoke through the numerous seers, like Kataribabo, Credonia Mwerinde and Joseph Kibwetere. Priests were warned against maligning the seers and referring to them as agents of the devil. By slandering the seers, priests were acting in the interests of Satan and thus hampering millions of people from joining the movement that God had chosen to steer them to eternal salvation.

Satan had taken a firm foothold on earth and had even managed to infiltrate the work that God entrusted to the priesthood. To drive Satan out of the world and chain him forever in hellfire required a priest to minister to his flock according to traditional rites and values that promote observance of the Ten Commandments. Yet a blind desire to change dearly held Catholic rites, such as penance, in order to accommodate modern earthly tastes, drove the Church and the priesthood deep into Satan's clutches.

The onus was upon each person of this generation to look for God when he could still be found and, most importantly, while still in the mood to show mercy to the sinner.

Father Kataribabo had recorded this encounter with Jesus Christ on audiocassettes. Interestingly Jesus had chosen to speak to him in Latin. At the Rugazi learning centre, Father Dominic Kataribabo's home base, these Latin tape recordings formed part of the induction course offered to cult aspirants.

Besides Joseph Kibwetere, Credonia Mwerinde and Dominic Kataribabo, numerous apostles of the ***Movement for the Restoration of the Ten Commandments of God*** claimed many more divine revelations. Included among the long list of seers were Scholastica Kamagara and her husband John, Charles Byaruhanga, Henry Byarugaba, Steria Kyakunzire, Jane Kasande, the Reverend Father Paul Ikazire and Credonia's sister Ursula Komuhangi. Christ and Mary, it was claimed, had the habit of entering these people and whichever one was possessed would speak to the awe-filled congregation.

Ursula Komuhangi claimed to have had initial contact with the Virgin Mary and Jesus while still a secondary school student, long before she abandoned school to link up with her older sister in the Nyamitanga compound of the Gaudia Kamushwa cult. Then the Virgin Mary had appeared to her, instructing her to leave school and embark on the Lord's mission, which was to evangelise among the youth. Her duty was to steer the youth away from their sinful ways and encourage them to observe the Ten Commandments. To her was revealed the kind of sinful laissez faire life-style that tended to entrap the youth, taking their attention away from strict observance of the Ten Commandments.

Through Ursula, Christ and the Virgin Mary instructed the youth to show obedience to their parents and church leaders. Ursula claimed to have been told by the Virgin Mary that promiscuity, fuelled by the knowledge of birth-control pill and condom availability, was widespread among young people. In spite of all these artificial barriers against procreation, the rate of unwanted pregnancies remained on the rise. Inevitably, this led to a high rate of abortions. Therefore, the Lord God through his humble child, Ursula, commanded that the youth lead a chaste life and abstain from sex before marriage. Those who practised artificial contraception or those in the business of procuring abortions had to live with the knowledge that they were breaking the Fifth Commandment.

Use of cosmetics and wearing fancy hairstyles were also strictly forbidden by the Virgin Mary. "*Be happy with your body, which is the temple of the Lord; for your body was created perfect and you should not use corrupt earthly standards to judge its beauty*," so spoke the Virgin Mary to Ursula. The Lord God had sent AIDS into the world as chastisement for rampant fornication, particularly among the youth. In the past there were many chaste youths from whose ranks the Lord God appointed angels and saints. But the rarity of virginity at the present time means that not many are able to join the ranks of angels and saints. If young people did not repent and reject immoral and shameful lifestyles, God would send even more severe punishments.

Ursula's final message to the youth after her apparition was, "*Let us join hands with the Blessed Virgin Mary, our Mother, and with our Lord Jesus Christ in the struggle against Satan by obeying the Ten Commandments. It is only through unity that*

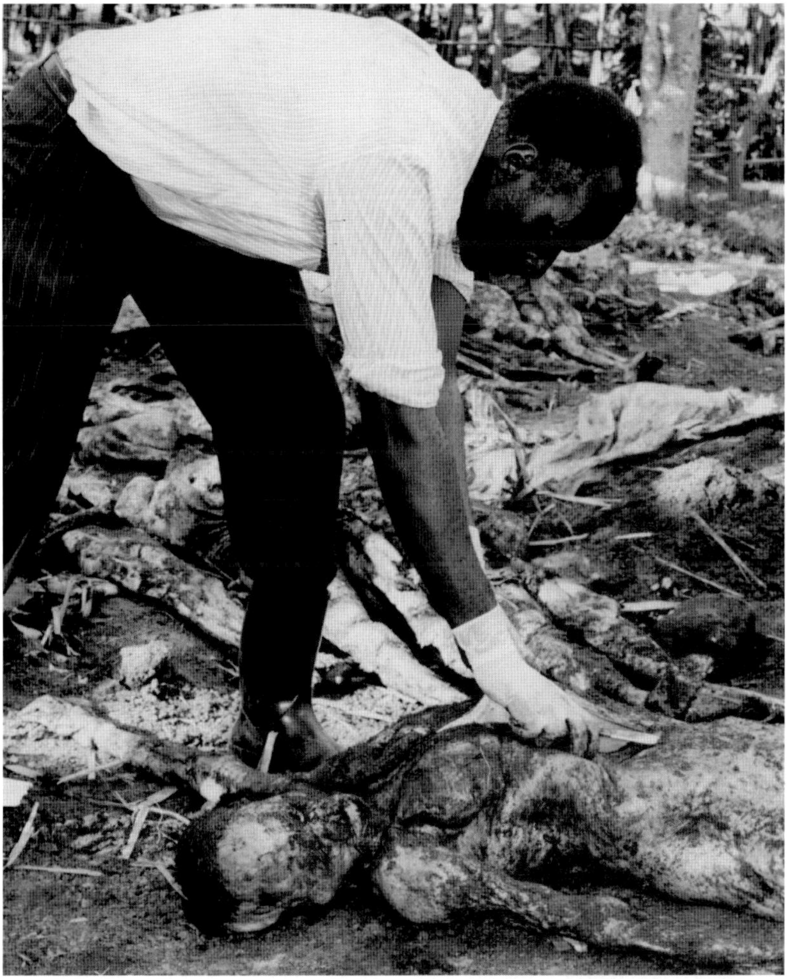

(top)
A forensic expert going through the charred remains of the dead.

(right)
Cover page of the cult's spiritual book

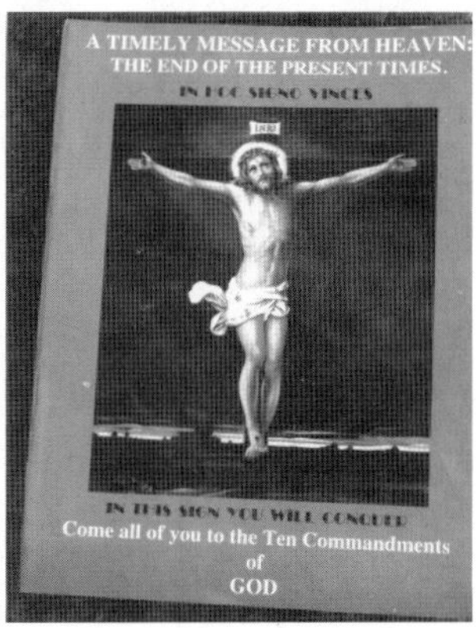

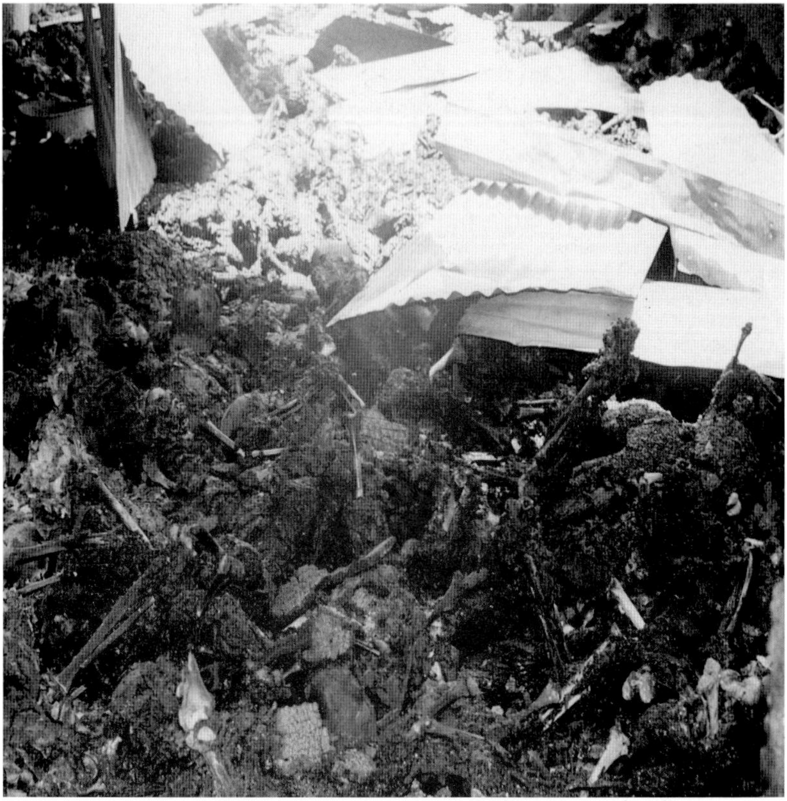

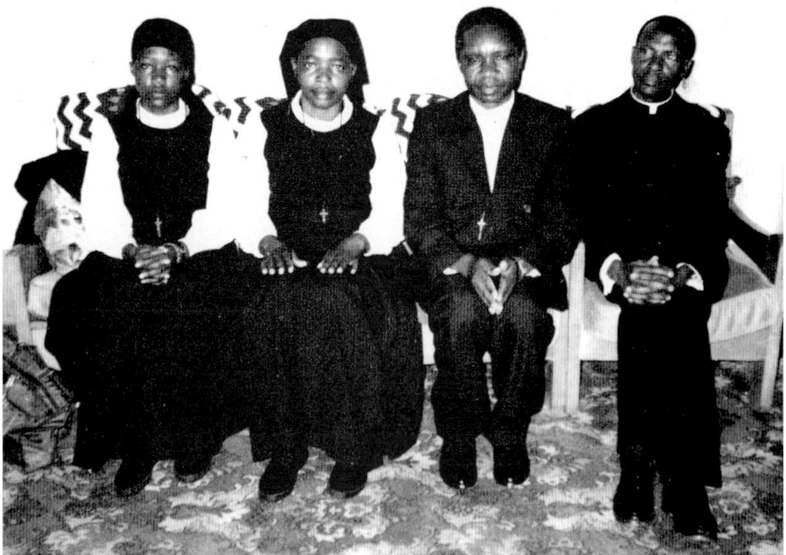

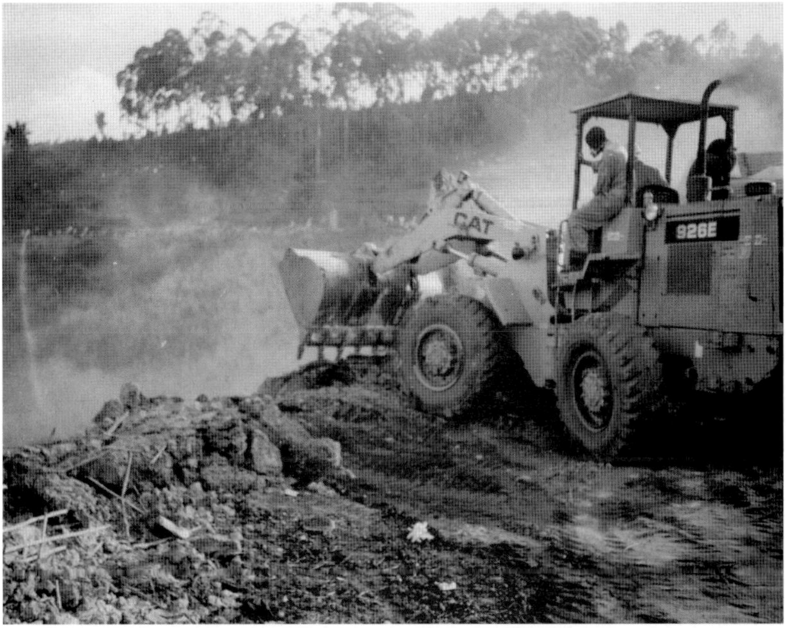

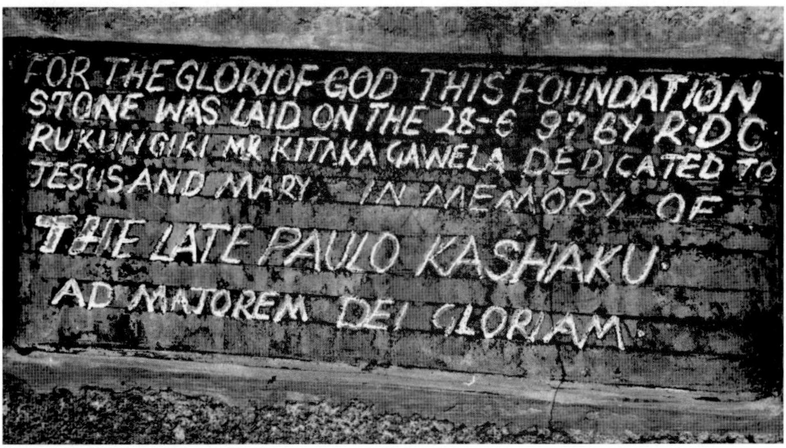

(from top left to bottom right)
A tangle of charred remains in the burned down chapel.
The key cult leaders. From left Ursula Komuhangi, Credonia.
Bulldozers covering the mass graves.
The foundation stone of the cult's primary school, which was dedicated to Jesus Christ, the Virgin Mary and Credonia Mwerinde's father.

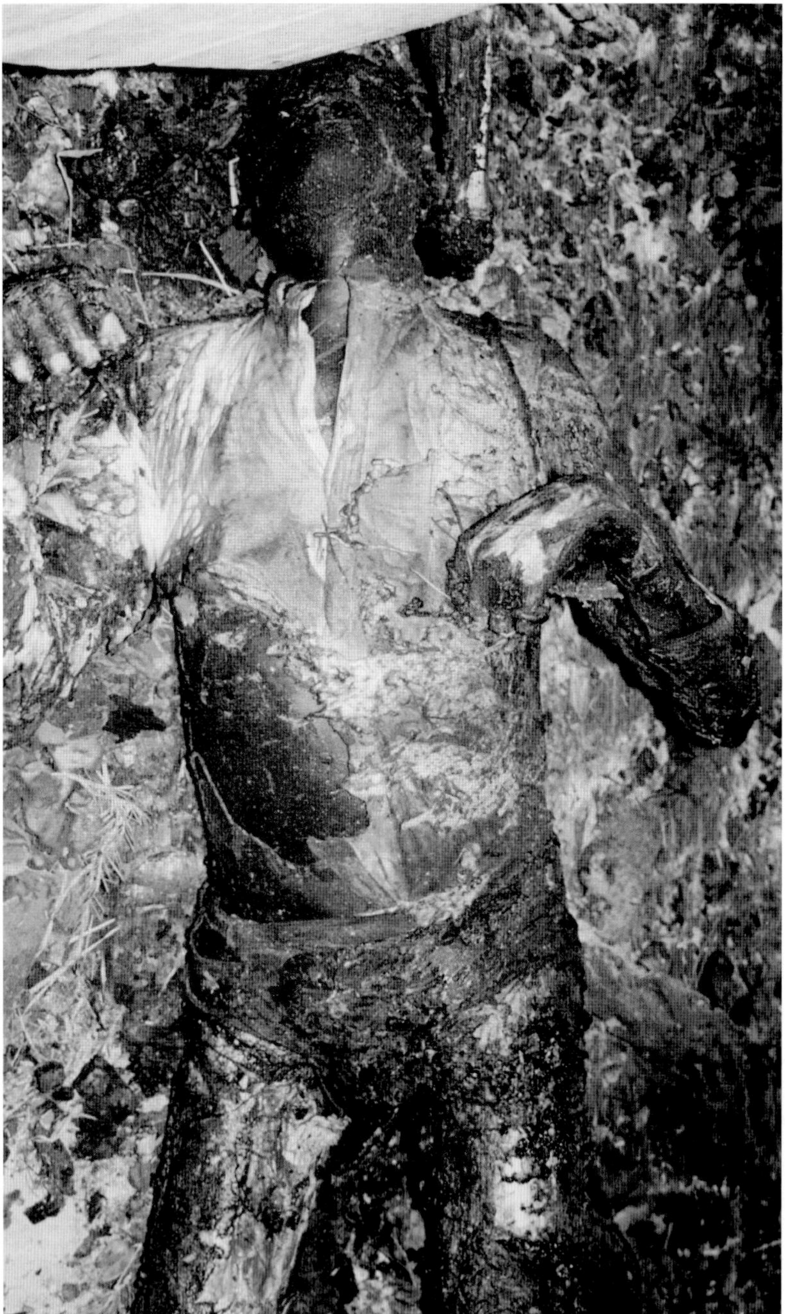

Close up of a charred body in the cult's church

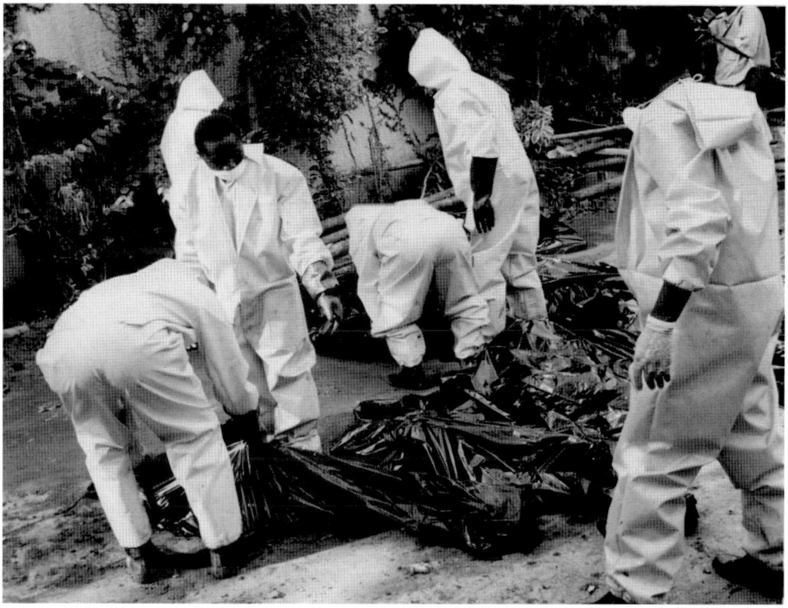

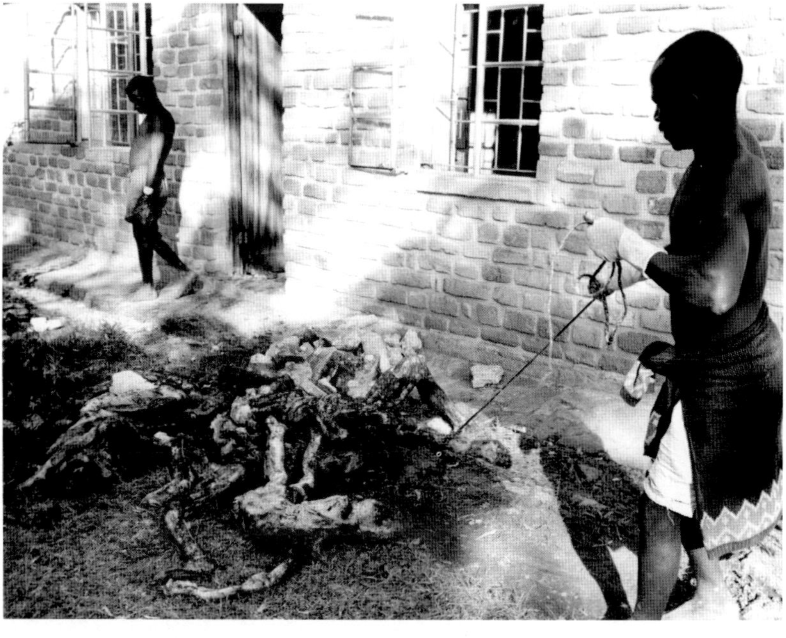

(from top to bottom)
Gruesome task of collecting the bodies of the dead
More bodies unearthed at another cult compound

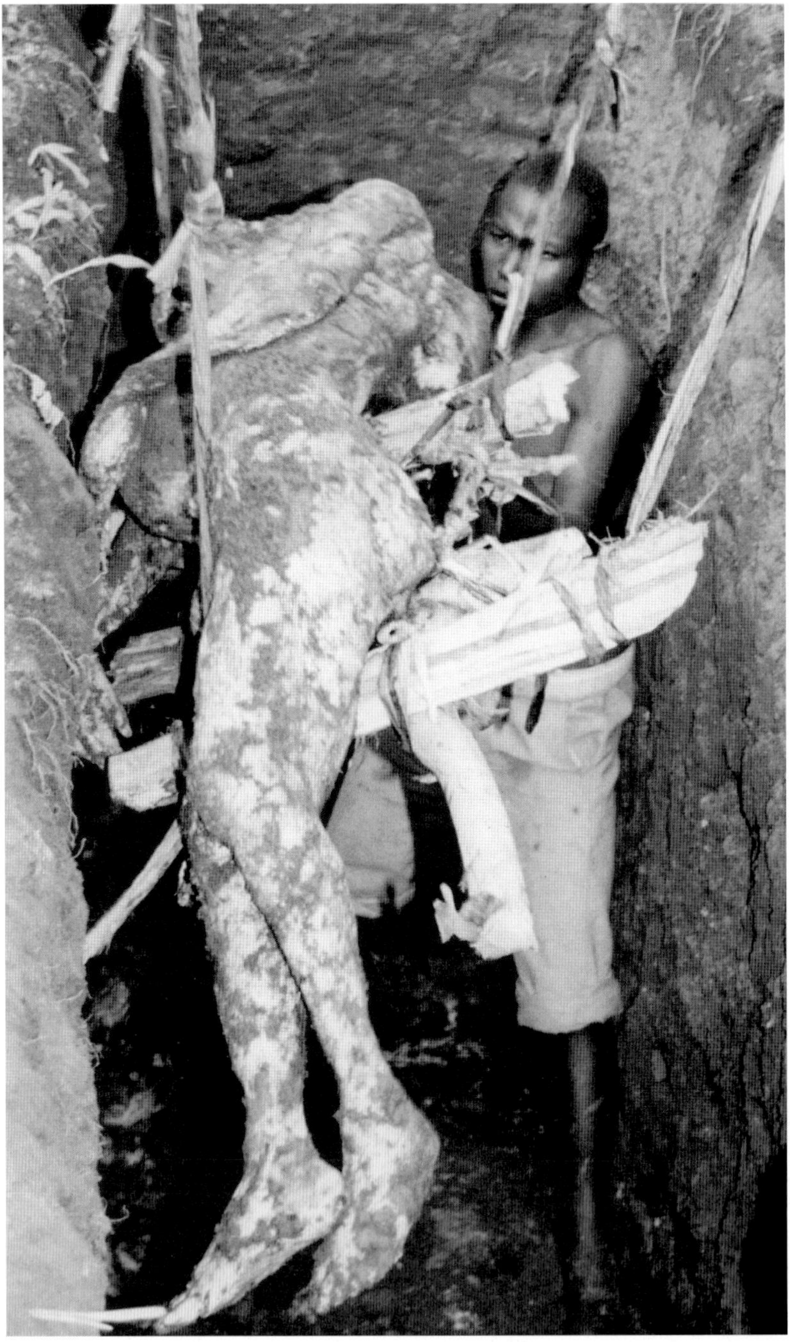

Lowering a body into a mass grave

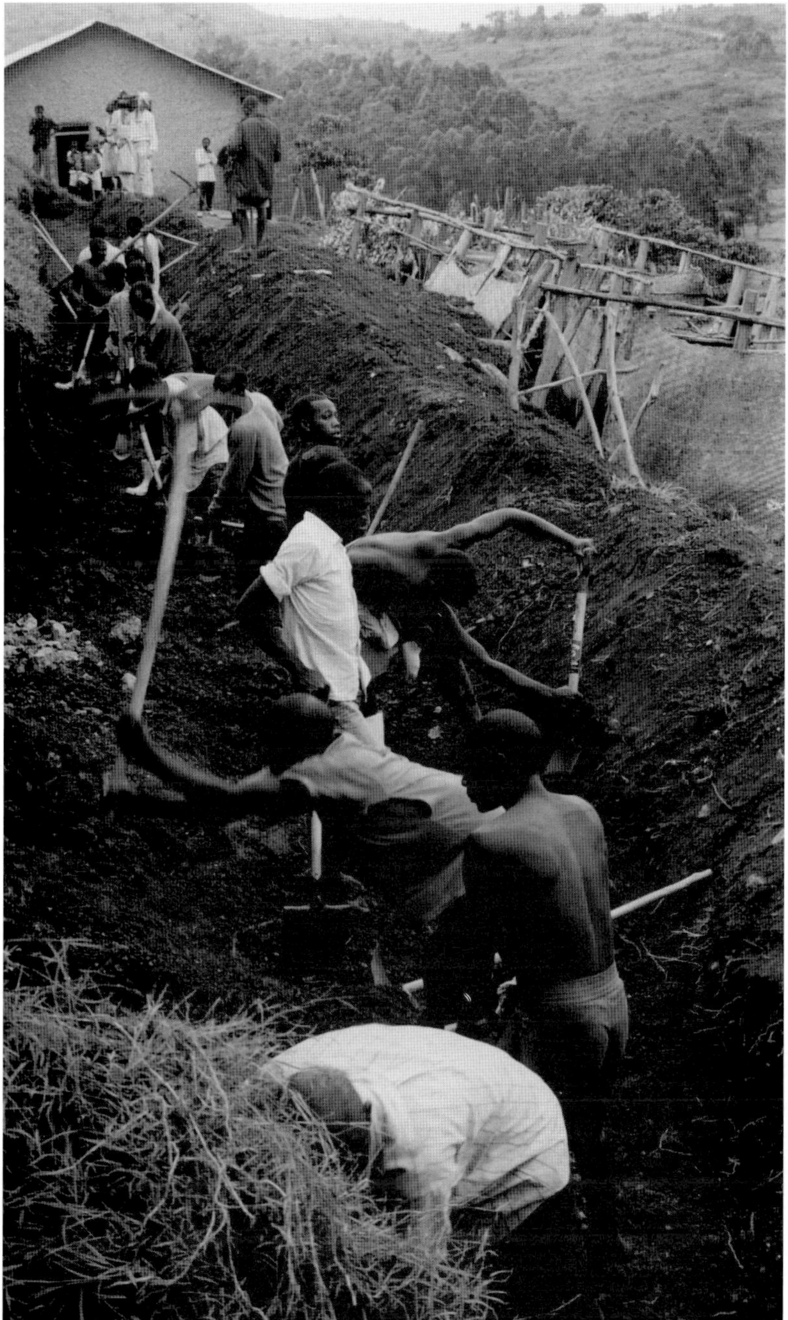

Prisoners digging a mass grave for the cult victims

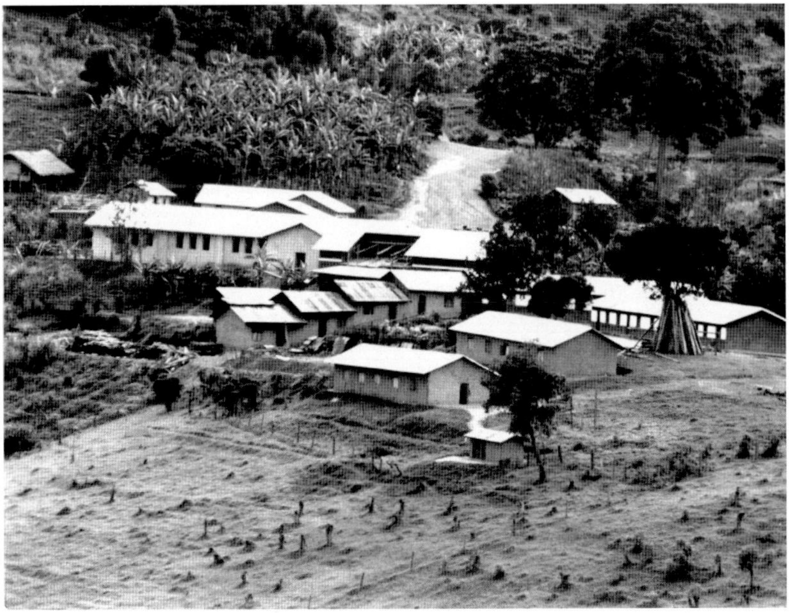

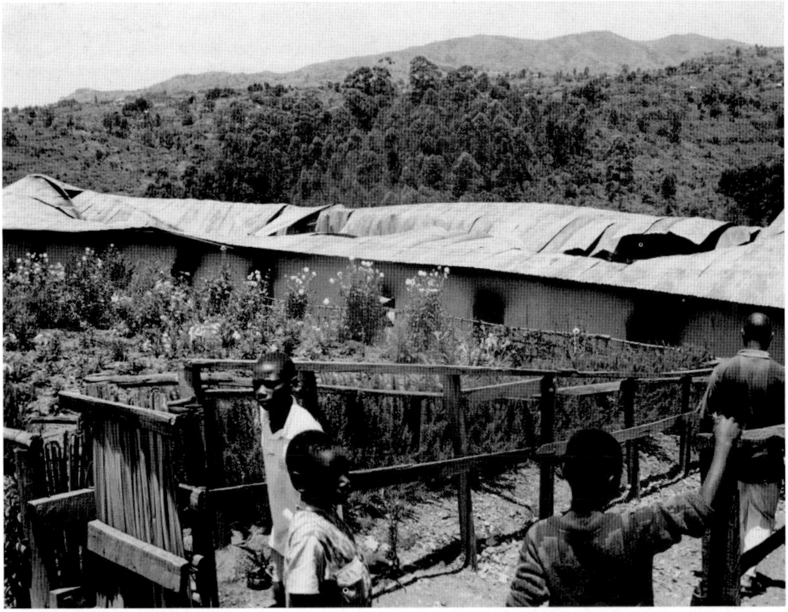

(from top to bottom)
The cult's compound at Kanungu
What remained of the cult compound after the inferno

we, the youth, can reclaim our rightful inheritance in God's Kingdom where we will live forever and ever. Repent and urge friends and family to convert to the ways of the Lord."

The cult's teachings were also inspired by seers from other parts of the world claiming to have had apparitions of the Virgin Mary in which she revealed a vision of the end of times. Greatly admired in cult circles was William Kamm, also known as the "Little Pebble". The Little Pebble is an Australian with claims of being in direct contact with the Madonna, Jesus Christ and lots of angels and saints. Other persons greatly revered by the Kibwetere movement included Padre Pio, Sister Rose Colomba Asdente, Sister Palma D'Oria, and Sister Marie Mantel. All were Italian members of Roman Catholic religious orders. Also admired was the Belgian Jesuit priest, Father Nectou. From France, Marie Baourdi, a Carmelite nun, was source for great spiritual inspiration as well.

Some of these people were regarded as dissidents within their orders but that didn't diminish their standing among the followers of the Kibwetere group. The prophecies of these "foreign" seers were of great interest to the Uganda group, serving to prove to their followers that indeed the world was on the verge of coming to an agonising end. According to cult teaching, Jesus Christ and the Virgin Mary had instructed the leaders to preach about the mystical experiences of the seers from abroad. These visions augmented those received by the Kibwetere group's own apostles. The soon approaching apocalyptic events were said to have been revealed to a number of cult seers, and they are briefly recounted below.

Tribulations of a magnitude hitherto unknown to mankind will be unleashed on those who have not repented and changed their ways to observe the Ten Commandments. A violent wind will arise in the east, uprooting giant trees and houses, and leaving in its wake a barren and desolate earth. More tornadoes and hurricanes will come and wash away dams. Then giant locusts shall descend upon the land and eat up those crops that would have survived the gale. Tired and famished, mankind will think, "We are smart. Why not eat the locusts?" Alas, the locusts will be poisonous and whoever tastes these insects will be brought to a slow and painful death.

Those who happen to have food stored in their homes might think themselves lucky. But they will not have counted on the devils descending upon them with a degree of aggressiveness never seen before. The little fiends will grab food out of their mouths. And when sinful man thinks that he has ammunition enough to shoot at the devil, he will fail to marshal enough energy to stand because of affliction with end-stage AIDS. With famine ruling supreme, cannibalism will become widespread. Mother will eat daughter and father will eat son.

For, while seeing these visions, a voice speaking from heaven proclaimed to one of the Kibwetere group seers, "*This is the end of sin. It is the end of this generation and time to punish those who refused to observe the Ten Commandments*." Not even the rich landowners with their great herds of cattle were spared. Prize bulls and cows were struck by lightening and their carcasses turned into a mass of deadly poison.

Trying to find refuge by drowning in alcohol won't do either; alcohol will have turned into an instant killer. If there should be any living person doubting these prophecies then they must look at the pestilence around them. AIDS is already a sign that these things are soon approaching.

When the end approaches, snakes shall crawl from every nook and cranny. Snakes with a diameter ten times the size of a lorry will frequently be encountered. On the other hand, garden-variety snakes will not disappear altogether. Instead they will multiply and become more aggressive. Be warned that the potency of snake venom will increase more than hundred-fold. But the anointed ones, adherents to the Ten Commandments, will be spared these tribulations. The Kibwetere group seer to whom these apocalyptic apparitions were revealed then saw one serpent, which was close on the heel of another. Both serpents had come from the same country. The two snakes covered the entire land so that a person could hardly take one step without stepping on their most grotesque scary skin of pins and needles.

Then the children of this generation will hear a loud bang of a violent earthquake tearing through the very core of the earth. Mountains and valleys will be thrown asunder. Amidst a deafening roar, the valleys will try to take refuge in the mountains, while the mountains will be rushing into the sea. Clouds will fall from the skies squashing and suffocating sinners. Woe unto those who have rejected the Ten Commandments, for they will be caught in-between. It will be a most horrific death lasting many years. Many sinners will cry out, "O God, the pain is unbearable. Please do kill us." But no mercy will be shown. Thirsty, the sinner will want to drink. But the water in the river and lakes will have turned into poisonous blood. When these things that have been revealed to the twelve apostles finally happen, woe to the sinful woman heavy with child or nursing little ones; lion cubs and leopards will replace their tender little children and these fierce beasts will demand to be breast-fed.

The Lord God will lead his children through all these terrible times. The Lord God says, "*All peoples of this world open your ears and listen to your Lord. When the year 1999 is completed, the year that follows will not be 2000. Instead year 1999 will be followed by year 1. And it will begin with a new people—a new generation replacing the current one. Of those alive today, the number that will be counted among the new generation will depend on the number of people repenting and willing to live according to my Ten Commandments.*" And the Lord God went on to explain to a seer of the Kibwetere group that the people of the new generation of year 1 will be his chosen tribe to which he will give the name "redeemed". Happy are the redeemed, for the inheritance of eternal life is theirs. The unrepentant sinner will disappear at the end of year 1999.

Transformation from the old to the new generation will take three days, starting on 29th December. During those three days the lights will go out from the skies and a terrible fear will permeate the earth. The sun, the stars and the moon will not shine. Darkness will envelop the entire universe and no amount of artificial light will be strong enough to illuminate the blackness.

However, the Lord God had entrusted the seers of the Kibwetere group with special lanterns that could shine brightly during those three days of total darkness. Because of this the Lord God instructed the seers to inform all his children to search for strong houses to shelter during that long period of darkness. Further, the seers were instructed to make sure that the faithful kept enough food and other provisions in store during the period of blackness.

Places of shelter would be built at sites where Jesus Christ and his mother had been appearing to the seers. The locations of the houses of shelter had been chosen because the Lord God had proclaimed them holy and untainted from human corruption and sin. To the seers the Lord God had given more instructions on the exact location of the houses. These shelters shall be known as "arks". Just before the three days of darkness three holy beings would instruct the seers to gather all the faithful in the arks.

Darkness would transform any living thing, man or beast, which remained outside the arks into devils. For those who stubbornly refused to repent, their end was guaranteed at the end of 1999.

After the three days of darkness the chosen people would wake up to a new day and a new start in a world free of sin and liberated from Satan. The new earth would be so beautiful and extremely flat—like a football field. The Lord God let one of the seers of the Kibwetere group see the new earth coming down from heaven. It contained every good thing, spiritual and material, necessary for the wellbeing of mankind.

Cheerful and healthy children played in the lush flat fields and their satisfied parents looked proudly on. Each family had a house with electricity and running water. No longer would people, especially women and children, have to walk miles in search of water. Neat glistening streets would replace the current dusty trails. And on the new earth husband and wife shall know no quarrels. Because AIDS and all other diseases would have been conquered, hospitals and doctors were totally unnecessary on the new earth. The seer was also shown a highway that connected the new earth to heaven. And whenever one of the redeemed wanted to make the journey to heaven all they needed to do was to step into a free vehicle and off they zoomed to regale in the company of angels and saints.

It is on basis of these supposedly mystic experiences that Kibwetere and his twelve apostles travelled much of western Uganda preaching to hundreds to repent and return to strict observance of God's Ten Commandments. The vast majority of Ugandans who heard Kibwetere or his apostles preach shrugged their shoulders when told fantastic stories of apparitions. After all, Ugandans had witnessed an explosion of new religious teachings in every corner of the land, promising better times either here on earth or in the kingdom to come.

As for the likes of Kibwetere and his zealots, they had seen many before. Ordinary folk just wanted to get on with their task of scratching a decent living in the geographical location called Uganda and were content in the fact that God ought to be left in his heaven, for humanity (including the so called seers) was too stupid to understand his ways.

Didn't Ugandans vividly recall a certain Yowanina Nanyonga who fooled the nation with her apparitions? Nanyonga, just like the Kibwetere group, claimed to have seen Mary. The Madonna appeared standing on a red anthill and handed her a simple remedy for AIDS. Whosoever wished to heal themselves of AIDS and other incurable diseases had to eat the soil taken from the anthill, which the Virgin had blessed. Thousands flocked to her for just a whiff of the soil. For some years there had been a lucrative trade in the soil that unscrupulous vendors claimed originated from the sacred anthill[39]. Needless to say, nobody got cured.

But even in the face of such evidence there was a section of the population that was convinced of the authenticity of men and women that claimed to be God's messengers, however ridiculous the tales of their apparitions and the punishments that supposedly awaited the non-believer. After Nanyonga there were many self-styled prophets that followed on the scene with claims bigger and grander. Therefore, it comes as no surprise that what Kibwetere and his apostles proclaimed touched some people profoundly. Not desiring to be like the proverbial seeds that landed on rock or in the marshes, they made haste and joined the cult.

Chapter 6
Seeking thy Kingdom

Instead, be concerned above everything else with the Kingdom of God and with what he requires of you, and he will provide you with all these other things. Matthew 6:33

As recounted before, the teachings and pronouncements of the ***Movement of the Restoration of the Ten Commandments of God*** might seem baseless and ridiculous to most fair-minded folk. But nevertheless there was a group of people who wholly embraced the seers and their apocalyptic message. The cult was careful to build most of its laws on a palatable platform that identified easily with prevailing religious and customary beliefs of the natives of western Uganda. Some morsel of indigenous belief flavoured with rudimentary passages from the Bible spiced the cult's end of time message.

Cult doctrine also built its moral and spiritual basis by pandering expertly to the fears, disillusionment and aspirations of largely poor and illiterate countryside folk. Given a countryside boasting a sizeable population of religious fence sitters at spiritual crossroads, bamboozled by the sheer diversity of religious brands flooding the ethereal market, the road to subjugation and total control of a people by callous spiritual leaders claiming visionary status was wide open. What led thousands to believe that salvation could be attained by following the teachings of the ***Movement for the Restoration of the Ten Commandments of God***?

It is important to emphasise that before the arrival of the cult on the Ugandan religious landscape, devotion to the Virgin Mary was and remains a common practice among Catholics. Opportunities abound to honour Mary as Mother of the Church. In August Catholics dedicate the entire month to honouring Mary's special role as the Mother of God and Queen of Heaven. By saying special prayers known as Novenas, believers can petition God through her.

The feast commemorating Mary's assumption, physically and spiritually, to heaven falls on 15th August. And on 22nd August the feast of the Immaculate Heart of Mary is celebrated. Of course, to most Ugandan Catholics, these feasts are not comparable to Christmas or Easter and may go unnoticed except among the more pious. For those wishing to cultivate a special spiritual relationship to Mary, there is the Legion of Mary that provides a legitimate and respectable platform to exercise that devotion[40] . The Legion of Mary is a popular movement especially among countryside folk.

Mary's appeal in Uganda, especially in the western parts of the country, extends beyond the bounds of the Catholic Church. Her reputation for revealing future events, mostly of a catastrophic nature conveyed through humble children and women, is an article of faith in much of Uganda, blurring denominational boundaries. In many Catholic parishes there are groups of enthusiasts that keenly keep track of places visited by the Madonna. For anybody wishing to read about the Virgin Mary's apparitions around the world there is more than enough literature in Uganda.

The Madonna has appeared in the remotest of places and in almost all countries since her first sighting at the beginning of the first century somewhere in Spain. Over twenty thousand apparitions, according to observers of the phenomenon, have been reported. Just near Mexico City, she showed herself to a simple peasant man. Many believed the apparition and subsequently converted. In Medjugorjie, Croatia, she appeared delivering a message that spoke of coming tribulations in the region. She is reported to be a constant visitor to the Australian visionary known as the "Little Pebble" and to whom she has promised the papacy[41] . With or without Church approval, Christians choose to believe all or some of the apparitions. And Ugandan Catholics do not behave any differently as testified by the story of our encounter with a Marian enthusiast and ex-Kibwetere follower, which is briefly recounted below.

Yokana Ndyanabo is a peasant farmer living with his wife and four children on a small piece of land in rural Uganda. To Yokana the Virgin Mary occupies a very special place in his life. This was evident on looking around the family's humble living quarters. Portraits of the Madonna were pinned all over the place. And around his neck he wore an oversized rosary. "This house is dedicated to the Immaculate Heart of Mary," he jovially informed us. He went on to tell us that if the Church ignored the messages that Mary continued to deliver to a select few around the world, then nations would be wiped off the face of the earth. To bring his point home he cited the February 2000 floods in Mozambique and the persistent wars in Africa as signs of the coming turmoil[42]. "That is only the beginning," he said as he ransacked through a wooden box that contained his precious collection of Marian literature. From its depths he excitedly retrieved what he termed "The mother of all good news". This turned out to be a broad sheet Marian publication dedicated to the Madonna's apparition to four children in the Spanish town of Garabandal sometime in 1961. He told us this was the latest edition of the publication, which he had recently got from one of the missionaries at the local parish.

It is widely held that when the Virgin Mary appeared to the four Spanish children she entrusted them with a message. Catholics were called upon to observe the sacrament of penance and make frequent visits to the Blessed Sacrament. Furthermore, they were instructed to lead morally upright lives. If these things were ignored then a chastisement would befall humanity. But before that cataclysm the Virgin Mary would appear again to some select people and warn them of the impending catastrophe. After the warning a miracle, visible to all mankind, would appear in the sky. And this would happen within twelve months of the warning. Yokana's excitement that led him to refer to the newest publication as the "mother of all good news" had to do with the fact that the newsletter revealed the month of the miracle. Indeed it was claimed the miracle would happen in April, and Yokana didn't think it important to know the year, which was conspicuous by its absence.

In western Uganda the Madonna's appearance in the Rwandan village of Kibeho and the prophecy of an approaching bloodbath in Rwanda is a common story. Because of its geographical and cultural proximity to Rwanda the people of western Uganda, more than their compatriots elsewhere in the country, followed closely in utter horror and disbelief at what some swore was the fulfilment of the Kibeho prophecy. In the summer of 1994 *interahamwe* militia went on a killing orgy. These men and women of extreme violence raped, maimed and killed with abandon. At the end of the killing spree, which took place in the full presence of a United Nations force, over one million people mostly Tutsi and moderate Hutu had been massacred. Their killers competed in bringing their victims to death by subjecting them to a most dehumanising and debasing treatment. *Interahamwe* brigands skewered their victims through the anal route and suspended the struggling helpless bodies over hot coals. Babies were decapitated and thousands were hacked to death. The atrocities are too numerous to recount here[43].

To the people of western Uganda and elsewhere that believed in the Kibeho apparitions there could be no better demonstration of fulfilment of a Marian prophecy. These people were convinced that if heed had been paid to the Madonna's message at Kibeho, which required leading the Rwandan nation through a period of fasting and prayer as atonement for its sins, and the content given the serious attention it deserved, the genocide would never have happened. It is a compelling story that sends a shiver down people's spines. Thereafter, anyone claiming a vision from the Virgin Mary was likely to be taken more seriously by lots of people in the region, irrespective of their religious inclinations. We must hasten to add that after the 1994 Rwanda genocide, devotion to Mary in the western parts of Uganda actually increased. In this region the trans-denominational nature of Mary is very much present, surpassing that of any other revered icon in the Christian world. So when the cult made the Virgin Mary the centrepiece of its teaching it had its calculations right; it was treading a well-beaten spiritual path.

Yokana Ndyanabo joined the cult just because it had restored the image of the Virgin Mary to a central place of honour in worship. He also believed that the Madonna had revealed herself to Kibwetere and the other apostles. Although he left the cult in 1997 he is still convinced that cult apostles had indeed seen Mary and her son. But because of their increasing pride and desire to accumulate material wealth, the devil had won them over. Sensing the hand of Satan in the Kibwetere group, Ndyanabo left. His biggest desire now is to visit Marian shrines in Europe, preferably in Garabandal. He believes that is where the end game between Satan and God will be played. Incidentally, the Garabandal Marian publication is courteous enough to publish a list of hotels and bed and breakfast facilities available in that town. For it is also believed that those who will be in Garabandal on that very day of the miracle shall automatically be saved.

Natives of the western parts of Uganda are no strangers to the phenomenon of apparitions. Encounters with supernatural beings and forces are an almost everyday experience here. Natives of this region firmly believe that gods had once ruled directly over their region. That was some hundreds of years ago. These rulers are the mythical Chwezi, greatly revered and feared to this day. Historians believe, with little evidence, that the Chwezi were Oromo tribesmen who trekked southwards to escape increasing pressure on land in their native Ethiopia. There are local historians who subscribe to the theory that these men were Roman soldiers who had somehow lost their way in the wilderness of central Africa. Whatever the truth may be, on pitching their tents in western Uganda the Chwezi established a peaceful dynasty.

The first Chwezi King, Ndahura, is said to have presided over a vast swathe of land stretching from north Uganda and extending into much of western Tanzania. The Chwezi were true miracle workers. And they were second to none in the Kingdom when it came to calling the spirits of the dead for a chat. With beads around their necks and waists and copper bangles around their arms and legs the Chwezi must have been quite a sight to the indigenous people. To add to their mystic quality the Chwezi bamboozled the locals with the display of lamps that burnt through much of the night. The likes of these lamps had never been seen in the region before.

Outside their spiritual feats they are believed to have been wise leaders with great compassion for their subjects. During the rule of the third Chwezi King, Wamara, the kingdom was hit by a series of misfortunes, including a long drought known locally as *Eijuga Nyoza*. This was sometime during the sixteenth century. In those pre-colonial days Africa's economy and therefore its social order was totally at the mercy of the climate. Being the considerate leaders that the

Chwezi were, their King took full responsibility for the misfortunes and abandoned the throne. According to local beliefs, the King and his fellow Chwezi then headed for Lake Victoria where they disappeared into its depths. It is on the basis of this account that natives of western Uganda believe that the Chwezi still live, albeit in another realm.

The spirits of the Chwezi dominate life in western Uganda and are the centre of a religious cult. We should note that these spirits are not viewed as the supreme God. Practitioners of the Chwezi cult believe that the supreme God, Rubare, goes about his heavenly chores with little interest in humans. He leaves the mundane tasks of running human affairs, such as handing out blessings or unleashing punishments, to spirits.

Worthy of mention is a northern Ugandan variation of the inactive God concept. Here too, although he often comes down to earth, God is somewhat disinterested in his creatures. The motives for His descent are rather sinister as He has this peculiar habit of eating people especially when He stumbles upon them at night[44] . Perhaps this is in reference to God's vengeful nature portrayed so vividly in the Old Testament. But we digress and so now we beg to return to the Chwezi, if you will.

Chwezi spirits, unlike the bodies from which they emanated, are believed to be in the business of causing human suffering and misfortune. Now and again they engage in demonic mischief and enter people. Possession by a Chwezi spirit manifests itself as physical or mental disease. If the spirits are not placated through worship and animal sacrifices they can be counted on to cause absolute mayhem. You, dear reader, and with all due respect to you, are perhaps tempted to protest, "But most cult followers were Christians. How then could they have allowed native pagan beliefs to influence their lives?" Well, we do not doubt that most cultists had belonged at one time to mainstream Christian churches that rant against indigenous African religious beliefs. The sooner we appreciate that in the African context, Christianity and other major religions of the world are complementary to existing traditional religious beliefs, the better for understanding the forces that led people to join the

Kanungu cult.

Undoubtedly, Christianity has influenced traditional African beliefs in a most profound way. On the one hand, this influence has led to the discarding of some of these values. On the other hand, traditional beliefs in the supernatural have impacted on the way that folk in Uganda (and much of Africa) understand and concretise the entire concept of Christianity and in particular its possibilities and limitations in explaining the place of the divine in human happiness and suffe-ring.

Many mainstream Christians might not be active members of the Chwezi religious cult and protest loudly if such an allegation were to be levelled at them. However, the reality of living in a region so dominated by the Chwezi in most aspects of day-to-day life suggests that the practice is rather different. The fear invoked by Chwezi spirits and their strong association with misfortunes in life drives many a Christian to come knocking at the Chwezi cult priest's shrine in search of answers to life's numerous vicissitudes. Since not much is known of the details of the relationship between heaven and earth, quite a few people decide to weather the spiritual storm by praying to both Christian and Chwezi deities.

Christian church leaders are definitely not amused by such dou ble allegiance, as we might surmise. "Give unto the Chwezi deity what is theirs and unto God what is his," underlines the tough Church position. The Church advises her own not to run to the shrines in cases of suspected Chwezi spirit possession, for the Church is fully capable of dealing with such mischievous spirits.

Interestingly, Father Dominic Kataribabo's credentials in extracting Chwezi spirits out of his demon-possessed parishioners were impressive. There are some who joined the Kibwetere cult because of a desire to distance themselves forever from these malevolent dark forces of long dead Roman legionaries (if we are to believe our local historian). Tales of the unique powers bestowed upon Father Dominic Kataribabo were enough to send them into the cult.

In that other non-human dimension, the Chwezi are believed to be the proud owners of large herds of cattle. But for some strange reason they prefer to forcibly employ men and women of flesh and blood to look after their sacred cows with the long horns. They get their human labour through abductions. These spiritual beings conduct their abduction missions at remote spots, especially during the night if one is foolhardy enough to be out and about without human company. It is not unusual to encounter people who fervently claim to have been held captive by the Chwezi in their spiritual world.

It is also claimed that these spirits enjoy lounging around springs and at certain times of the year, just when the sun is about to set, they can be seen bathing in the sparkling water. Western Uganda is awash with countless tales of Chwezi apparitions and abductions. So, when Kibwetere and colleagues begun talking about apparitions, it was not an unreasonable claim under the circumstances.

It is instructive to note that the cult emerged at a time when AIDS was devastating Uganda. Of all epidemics to hit this central African region, and there have been numerous, none has heaped such grinding misery on the population. It is hard to find a family that has not lost a dear one to the dreadful disease. At the end of the millennium the number of deaths attributed to the disease was a staggering one million.

Most of the affected are people in their prime. Opening a Ugandan newspaper drives the point home. Most of the pages are devoted to obituaries of young men and women who have met their demise following "a long illness", a local euphemism for AIDS. In short, the disease hits the most productive in society.

But the very young are not spared either. Babies might get infected while still in the womb or at delivery. And it is near miraculous if they survive long enough to celebrate their fifth birthday. The extended family network tries to support the millions of AIDS orphans but with little success. When young parents die, their children are often looked after by mostly poor grandparents, who, paradoxically, had counted on the support of their own children to see them through old age. Often this means that there will be no money to send orphans to a school that can provide them with a decent education and hope for a better future. Clearly, the extended family network was not built to shoulder a burden of this magnitude. Little wonder, then, that it has begun to show deep cracks.

Faced with a ferocious epidemic that seems to rob young lives at will, people seek answers. They would like to understand from whence came this incurable disease and why it appeared at this particular time in history and how best they could avoid being caught up in its deadly jaws. Reasonable people might be quick to point out that AIDS is caused by a virus, transmitted, by and large, during sexual intercourse. Not so, retort dissenting voices. AIDS, according to cult teaching, was a curse from God. For the Lord God looked down upon fornicating humans and he was deeply offended; mankind had thrown the Sixth and Ninth Commandment to the winds. Thus, it was only right and fitting to punish the sinners.

During her alleged meeting with the Madonna in 1989 Credonia Mwerinde had been referred to the Bible in order to get an even firmer basis for understanding the spiritual origins of the disease. It was to be found in Leviticus 26:14-26 and partly reads, "*If you refuse to obey my laws and commands and break the covenant I have made with you, I (the Lord) will punish you. I will bring disasters on you—incurable diseases and fevers that will make you blind and cause your life to waste away*." Further, cult teaching warned that scientists might work hard at their laboratory benches trying to get a cure, but alas, the only tangible result for all these misdirected efforts would be hundreds and thousands of broken test tubes and no cure in sight.

In a message delivered by the Virgin Mary and Jesus Christ to one Henry Seempa, another apostle of the ***Movement for the Restoration of the Ten Commandments of God***, mankind was told of ways to cure itself of AIDS. The Lord God pronounced that mankind's effort to find a cure for AIDS would amount to naught. But to the seers of the Kibwetere group, the Lord had handed medicine. However, this highly potent medication could do its job only when the sick or those that sought immunisation remained faithful to the Ten Commandments. The healing power of the sacred medicine, which the movement would supposedly distribute free of charge, was in direct proportion to one's faith in the message preached by the cult. And anyway, cautioned the seer, it was far better to avoid catching AIDS in the first place by not breaking the vital Sixth and Ninth Commandments—violation of which led to the disease. Evidently, prevention was to be preferred to cure.

Gripped in the fear of a disease with a propensity of reducing those who were fat as pigs (a sign of good health and well being in this region) to skin and bone, the people saw salvation in the cult's divinely inspired messages. In a sense one can argue that by playing the AIDS card the cult was taking full advantage of mankind's inner quest for self-preservation and propagation of the species. Without a doubt there was a Darwinian flavour to it.

Another factor that helps us gain some insight into the reasons that led hundreds to sign up with the Movement for the Restoration of the Ten Commandments of God can be found in the government's dismal performance in raising the standards of living for rural folk on one hand and the charisma of the cult leadership on the other. Of course, Uganda is not Kampala—the country's capital. In the absence of evidence to the contrary, we are cautious about making such a shameful allegation. But we are acutely aware that for any Ugandan aspiring to be somebody, Kampala and not some backwater of western Uganda is the place to be.

Because of this, the people that count on the politico-economic landscape are based in the capital. Naturally, but unfairly, a lion's share of investments goes to Kampala. All governmental departments and the best schools and hospitals are to be found in there. Kampala is booming after many years of decline. A high concentration of second-hand cars negotiating the pot-holed streets discharging thick clouds of black exhaust fumes is visible testimony to this prosperity. The countryside is only courted when some form of election is at hand. Then the well-to-do aspirants for high office remember their brethren in the villages. With free cigarettes and free paraffin for the routinely empty lamps, the peasants are bribed into choosing the men and women who will go on to the legislature in Kampala to "eat the national cake on their behalf"—local Ugandan political parlance referring to this system of naked opportunism.

Since coming to power in 1986 Mr. Museveni's government has been continuously engaged in some sort of military expedition. Numerous groups, particularly in the northern region, have waged war against the NRM government ever since it came to power. However, none of these bands of internal dissidents are fighting for some cherished universal goal such as the establishment of a genuine democratic society, although the country could greatly benefit from better governance[45] . In fact the leaders of these guerrilla movements are some of the most vicious and violent men alive today. Maiming children and raping with abandon seems to be more like their cherished dream.

As if engaging these rebels wasn't enough, the Museveni government invaded the Democratic Republic of the Congo. The official government position was that this invasion was necessary to protect Uganda's security and sovereignty. Pundits begged to disagree and cited diamonds, gold and antique relics (aplenty in the Congo) as the real motive for a war that always had a potential of creating the worst humanitarian disaster in the Great Lakes region of Africa, overshadowing even the 1994 Rwanda genocide. At least two United Nation's reports have detailed Uganda and Rwanda's role in the plundering of the Democratic Republic of the Congo, a charge that both countries dismiss[46] .

Be they in the Congo or within the country, these senseless wars of attrition have claimed the lives of many soldiers in their prime. And most of the victims tend to originate from western Uganda. Because most top politicians in Uganda are from the west of the country, it is also natural (according to the logic of that unique African affliction called tribalism) to rely mostly on soldiers recruited from the same region. Total and unquestioning loyalty is easy to come by from home-boys, so the warped reasoning goes. Therefore, when the military engaged in rather messy and bloody battles inside and outside the country, deaths of soldiers from the western regions tended to be over-represented. Sadly, it is these very soldiers that countryside kin and kith had come to rely on for financial support.

It cannot be over-emphasised that on many scores the government has marginalised the peasantry, helping to create the all too familiar image that people have come to associate with life in Africa: rampant disease, famine, distressing squalor and monumental ignorance. Keen to escape from a meddlesome government all too quick to tax but with cold feet when it comes to delivering services, some people were keen to jump on a bandwagon promising better days. And that was what the cult came to symbolise in the eyes of some.

We were told of a woman, a mother of five, whose husband had been deployed to fight the evil Lord's Resistance Army of Joseph Kony in the north of Uganda. Just as his battalion was pursuing the last of the worn-out rebels into southern Sudan, the unit was ordered to deploy immediately into the Congo, where he was mortally wounded during a fight that saw two former allies (Rwanda and Uganda) fighting each other. On receipt of news of her husband's death this woman collapsed in disillusionment and despair. She had nobody to turn to. Angry at her helplessness and inability to correct what she viewed as an unjust system of earthly governance, she began re-examining the entire meaning of life. It is around that time of great grief and total uncertainty that she stumbled on the seers.

She didn't hesitate when she heard the message. It was the truth. In pursuance of that deeper truth, and true understanding of the meaning of life and her role in God's greater design for humanity's salvation, she joined the cult. At first it gave her comfort from the unsympathetic world and it soothed her anguished soul. One year later, just a few months before the cult fell in disrepute, she had the good sense to leave after noting that the leadership took no account of the well-being of their members.

When her daughter fell sick with a high fever, shaking chills and convulsions, she could not take her to see a doctor. Credonia Mwerinde insisted that the child be taken to the sacred Nyabugoto rock instead. Not prepared to lose another person so dear to her, she took her children out of the cult compound, amidst threats from cult leaders, and headed straight to a dispensary where her ailing daughter received proper treatment. The next time she heard about the cult was when they had burned over five hundred followers to death and the death toll was still rising.

Father Paul Ikazire, ex-cult priest (but now back to the mainstream) claims to have joined the cult as a means of forcing the Catholic Church re-examine the moral decay that threatened to eat it up, soul and all. There were some Catholics who were completely disillusioned by the behaviour of their priests and catechists. Increasingly, they saw their clergy as seekers of worldly pleasures with little interest in promoting Church teachings. Scandalous affairs involving the men of God are standard tabloid fodder in Uganda. In spite of claims of celibacy, quite a few Catholic priests have been caught with their pants down. A parishioner who finds his priest or lay minister of the church tumbling in the hay with his wife is likely to reconsider receiving sacraments from the voracious pleasure hunter.

There was another group of people who could not cope with the new changes that had been cropping up in the Catholic Church. Since the convention of the second Vatican Council by Pope John XXIII the wheels of Rome had moved with unaccustomed speed. Many of these changes, mostly over patterns of ritual at mass, were unpalatable to some Catholics in the Uganda countryside. For example, Latin gradually gave way to local languages during mass. And much to their chagrin, individual confession was replaced by general penance. In the past, Saturday afternoons were reserved for confession. But now nobody bothered to kneel before a priest and recount the litany of sins committed during the week.

As if this were not enough, the ritual of receiving the body of Christ had been modified to suit modern tastes. People no longer received the host on their tongues but put forward their dirty hands to receive the living body of Christ. Even then, they received this all-important communion not on their knees but standing as if waiting their turn at a public lavatory. Thus disgruntled, these people found lots of sense in Kibwetere's message that ranted against such satanic practices.

At the centre of the cult was a charismatic leadership. In a certain sense Kibwetere and his apostles filled a leadership vacuum created by a government that had virtually deserted the countryside. Through past deeds Kibwetere had shown himself to be a successful leader and entrepreneur. During his youthful days he had spearheaded education in the region. In retirement he had shown that Ugandans were capable of running a commercial farm and with success. Even before he became obsessed with visions Kibwetere's farm was the envy of many. To the peasantry the man did not have to prove himself. He could be counted on to deliver on his promise.

As for Father Kataribabo, he was respected as a good Catholic priest. He was just the kind of man worthy to have as one's parish priest. Besides, he was against any attempts at modernising the church. This was a stand that went down well, especially among a group of older, conservative Catholics in the parish. Also, the mere fact that he had obtained his doctorate in the United States added sevenfold to his credentials. In front of the peasantry, Father Kataribabo could claim a certain degree of monopoly over knowledge, particularly of a spiritual nature.

People in Kanungu could probably find it easier to dismiss Credonia since she did not have a reputation of being a morally upright person. But this is not how those originating from outside Kanungu viewed her. To them she was the personal friend of the Madonna and her son. It is because of this friendship that she was taken on a tour of heaven, hell and purgatory to witness these places at first hand and return with a message of salvation for those that Satan had not marked with the triple six symbol of destruction. She was the earthling with mystical experiences that she seemed to repeat at will, rather in the fashion that some people walk to a switch and turn the light on and off. It was to this trio of Joseph Kibwetere, Father Dominic Kataribabo and Credonia Mwerinde that followers turned to, to fill the vacuum not only in their spiritual lives but also to equip them with the means to cushion themselves against the rough and tumble of the reality that defines life in a typical Ugandan village.

Kibwetere and his comrades-in-the-spirit didn't talk about some highflying fancy project like quality education for all, a painfully familiar promise from many a politician's mouth. The cult leadership was a smart lot, capable of discussing their agenda on the same level as their audience. For example, take one of the messages that the Virgin Mary delivered to one of the cult visionaries on cats. The Madonna ordered the seer to warn all her children not to keep cats. Satan had chosen to hide in these fluffy innocent-looking animals as a tactic of getting closer to people and tempting them.

This was not a nonsensical claim snatched from out of the blue. Along the East African coastline, where belief in dark supernatural forces runs even deeper than in the heartland, not all cats are thought to be cats. Most cats seen lazily dozing the afternoon away in the humid Indian Ocean breeze of a city like Mombasa or Malindi are said to be naughty spirits. At nightfall they disguise themselves as beautiful women. Once transformed the spirits hit the neon-lit streets on a seductive hunt, swivelling their waists as if they were high society call girls, calling at night-clubs and other houses of pleasure. These spirits reputedly never rebuff a proposition. But after their victim has satisfied his lust, he falls into a deep slumber only to wake up in a graveyard the next morning surrounded by a curious crowd of jeering spectators pointing at his nakedness. This is a common tale in the region and there are those that believe every single word of it.

Therefore, when the cult instructed its followers not to keep cats because of their supposed evil nature, there was nothing strange about that. The message just went to confirm what people had suspected all along. Just in case you end up in one of those ghost-infested dingy places and have trouble distinguishing between a real beauty and the phoney, take heart. According to local experts on this phenomenon, phoneys walk about without shadows which, by the way, might be true of most people under a nocturnal African sky.

Chapter 7
The faithful

For God's promise was made to you and your children, and to all who are far away—all whom the Lord our God calls to himself. Acts 2:29

Before admission into Kibwetere's group, prospective members had to enrol for a special program meant to clothe them in spiritual armour strong enough to repulse the devil even at his worst. The idea of conducting these courses was a brainchild of none other than the Madonna, the cult leadership claimed. It is not clear when this message was delivered but what is certain, according to cult accounts, is that the Virgin Mary revealed herself to Scholastica Kamagara, a female apostle of the Kibwetere movement, handing down elaborate instructions that governed recruitment of new members. Upon expression of interest to join the movement aspirants were ordered to report every Monday and Friday to the learning centres which were staffed by seers rich in the knowledge of guiding the sinful to a worthy place in paradise.

The Virgin Mary had chosen Mondays and Fridays because these were the days when Christians were expected to fast. Satan, it was argued, was really scared of confronting fasting people. Accordingly, aspirants were urged to attend courses on an empty stomach. Instructions in cult teachings began at eight o'clock in the morning and ran through till four o'clock in the afternoon. At each session names of attendees and their reporting time were noted. Soon-to-be cultists were told the list would be handed over to the Virgin Mary. Dedicated aspirants who attended every session and arrived on time were told that the Madonna would reward them for their devotion. On the other hand the Virgin Mary would interpret truancy as insubordination to her divine revelation, a sin that she would punish most severely.

Once at the learning centre the first lesson was dedicated to general body hygiene. Keeping long hair or nails was condemned. And if there happened to be a female with painted nails, this practice was condemned in the strongest terms possible. Then the class was dismissed with instructions to attend to these matters of utmost spiritual importance. Hair was shaved and stored in a clay pot where it awaited an important ritual. Next time the class convened, their scalps were so shiny that you could see your reflection in them. Long dirty nails had all disappeared and the pubic area was clean-shaven as well. No whiff of perfume or scented soap could be discerned. Artificial fragrances were strictly forbidden since they alerted the devil of one's whereabouts.

Although aspirants didn't wear the standard cult uniform at this early stage, none would be admitted into the class if their dress was judged as shameful and disrespectful. Since males, save a few wearing tattered pants exposing patches of bare bottoms, were by definition decently dressed, the main targets of this condemnation were female aspirants. Of course, see-through dresses and garments exposing the female back or thigh were taboo. Skirts that went above the knees were not tolerated either. After defining the first rules of engaging the devil the class was now physically ready for spiritual instructions.

Emphasis was placed on denouncing material things of this world. Money and material property cannot stand the test of time, the seers told a class hankering after salvation. Eager not to miss the boat, aspirants outperformed each other in denouncing their right to property and handing it over to the cult. There is a story told of a young man who had died in the fire that raged through the cult compound on 17th March 2000. His family had tried to prevent him from selling all his earthly belongings and handing the money over to the Kibwetere movement. But the young man had astounded the family when he calmly pronounced, "I regret not having more cows to sell in order to raise even more money for the divine mission entrusted to our spiritual leaders." At this stage it appears that cultists had no qualms about the fact that the leaders were asking them to denounce right to own property.

Time was allocated for going through the Ten Commandments and a critical examination of the circumstances that led one to violate them. The highlight of the course, however, was reserved for a deeper study of the messages that the Virgin Mary delivered to numerous people around the world, including the group's own seers. For ten weeks aspirants wallowed in the wondrous world of supernatural manifestations and trembled at the coming tribulations—the ultimate price sinners have to pay for violating the Ten Commandments.

On completion of the training program aspirants underwent a ritual that symbolised rebirth into a new caste of God's chosen people. Coming this far was a moment to savour. It marked the beginning of a new life as a member of a new generation: a generation that would survive the soon-approaching three days of absolute darkness. The ritual didn't involve immersion in water or rubbing holy oil on the forehead. Inelegance of this nature was deemed too earthly. Once deemed a genuine believer and ready to take the plunge into the secretive inner world of the cult, it was required that the new recruits eat a concoction of burnt hair and human blood[47]. It was only then that the robes were issued, and the colours to be worn were in accordance with the amount of money or property that the individual had handed over to the cult.

Partaking in the ritual was an important rite of passage into the occult inner world of the organisation. For those judged to have performed exceptionally well during the courses or those favoured by the cult leadership for whatever reason, an extra special ceremony waited. This involved one of the cult apostles and the favoured person. Both made slits in the skin and mixed their blood together. It must be stressed here that this ceremony is not a cult invention. It is commonly practised in western Uganda and referred to locally as *omukago*. *Omukago* is a covenant entered into by two people as an expression of everlasting fraternity. It ensures an undying friendship that cannot be destroyed even by a roaring tropical fire in the dry season.

Much emphasis was put on training aspirants in the use of sign language, since opening one's mouth might inadvertently tempt one to break the Ten Commandments. It was also hammered into the cultists' heads that observance of total silence was a prerequisite if followers desired to get a message from the Blessed Virgin Mary or hear the voice of God. After the initiation ceremony the new tongue-tied members were encouraged to swap their homes for life in the cult's Kanungu compound.

Life in the compound could best be summarised as a combination of a rigorous prayer schedule characteristic of a monastery and merciless physical exertion typical of a hard labour camp. Movement outside the compound was only undertaken with express permission from one of the apostles. Interestingly, on those rare occasions when cultists ventured out of the compound to visit sick relatives or attend funerals they doggedly stuck to the rule of silence, much to the discomfort of their hosts.

Austerity defined life in the cult compound. The day began at four o'clock in the morning with a service that lasted four hours. And during each service, presided over by one of the ex-Catholic priests, there was the miracle of wine turning into blood. Unlike the case of Specioza Munkatabona, the prophetess who took western Uganda by storm, this was not a private miracle limited to one individual's experience. All who partook of the wine could taste blood in their mouths. Some former cult members insist the chalices were filled with human blood and not some innocuous drink like sheep or goat blood.

Ordinary cult followers were not party to the more interesting spiritual experience of apparitions, but being direct witnesses to this particular miracle meant they need not feel neglected in the shower of blessings that had rained upon their community. To most of the peasant followers of the cult, experiencing such a transformation was in itself beyond the limits of human explanation. If anything, this miracle must have helped them reaffirm their belief in the cult and its leadership. The cult leaders explained to their followers that this one miracle helped all who partook in the Eucharist to attain a higher and more powerful status. This was a prerequisite for the creation of a new spiritual being, superior to the mortal corporeal and unsullied by it.

Cultists were an obedient lot, toiling like donkeys and obsessed with worship. In between working the movement's farm, cultists were allowed short breaks of anything from fifteen to thirty minutes. But since the devil finds mischievous work for idle hands, these moments of rest were not empty either. One of the apostles would come up and deliver a sermon based on the previous evening's apparition. The general punch line of such a sermon focused on the coming suffering and tribulations of a fiery hell that would soon overwhelm and totally annihilate non-believers.

Sermons were alternated with recitation of the rosary, which was at the core of cult belief. Recitation of it on a daily basis was enforced. Besides, followers had to know its history. Familiarity with the fearful things that would befall one for paying little attention to this powerful instrument of prayer was emphasised.

The rosary as a central piece of cult belief, like most of cult doctrine, came about by divine revelation. Intriguingly it was to Theresa Kibwetere that this message was delivered[48] . Cultists were encouraged to recite the prayers on the rosary while kneeling. On the rationale of reciting the rosary, the Virgin Mary purportedly told Theresa thus, "*Wherever I go, I parade the rosary. Wherever I stand I make children recite the rosary. I proclaim the rosary everywhere because it is a powerful weapon for your salvation and to gain your graces.*" Then Mary had added, "*All the rosaries that you recite are gathered together by your guardian angels, who then bring them to me. At the moment of your death I will tie them around you and with my arms pull you to heaven.*"

Thus fired spiritually, the cultists were ready to resume their work on the farm. Clearing weeds, watering crops and collecting the harvest, cultists worked silently on the farm, like an army of red ants. Dinner was served late in the evening after attending another service. The refectory table reflected austere tastes. Children were fed on a thin porridge and lots of "holy water". No meat or poultry was ever served, in spite of its abundance on the farm.

Eggs and milk were sold to traders coming from Rukungiri, Mbarara and beyond. Kampala-based sons and daughters from the region, paying the countryside the obligatory once-in-a-blue-moon visit, could count on the cult farm as a source of cheap high-quality eggs and vegetables to whet their sophisticated urban appetites. Most people agreed that the farm manager, an ex-policeman answering to the name Kaganga, was one jolly good fellow who knew what it took to run a successful farm.

Just before repairing to bed there was time for more prayers in the Church. This was a fundamental part of spiritual formation in the cult compound and was very often presided over by one of the top three—Credonia Mwerinde, Joseph Kibwetere or Father Dominic Kataribabo. Again the latest news from heaven was communicated. Sinners would drown in high boiling seas and monstrous creatures would stalk the countryside in search of those who had rejected the Ten Commandments. Cultists were urged not to be afraid of the coming chastisements because they were already earmarked for redemption.

No doubt these apocryphal images of forbidding countenances were conjured up to frighten followers and ultimately keep them firmly in the clutches of the cult and its leadership. This was an important step on a path that would culminate in the total control of followers' thoughts and actions. Now and again tapes of one of the apostles talking in Latin to the Virgin Mary or Jesus Christ would be played. And the Latin-illiterate cultists would be awed and humbled by the experience.

At midnight the cultists finally went to their dormitories to snatch some sleep. There were men who had come with their wives. Such couples were not permitted to share the same bed and sexual unions were not tolerated either. It appears unions of this nature equated to fornication, which was portrayed by cult teaching as the most heinous of sins, even surpassing murder. There is a report of a man caught making love to his wife in the bushes that surrounded the cult compound. The couple was subjected to harsh punishment, which included flogging in the presence of other cultists[49]. Parents were also separated from their older children and there were wilful attempts to disperse family members by sending them to different cult camps.

Was the cult leadership made up of innocent bona fide visionaries? Or were the leaders phoney actors bound by one common thread—deceit? The sad reality is that for all their high moral sermons, it would be wrong to conclude that cult leaders were icons of Christian values and morality. Kibwetere and his inner circle of apostles preached austerity to others but allowed themselves the pleasures of this world. The cult's inner circle lived in separate quarters, away from the huge dormitories housing their followers. Nightlife in their quarters would fill many a regular night club patron with envy. There was music and dancing, and large trays of roast goat and beef were passed round among the partying cultists. Apart from an assortment of alcoholic beverages, it has been claimed by various sources that human blood was also available for the drinking pleasure of those attending the evening feasts.

For some strange reason human flesh popped up on the list of delicacies served during these macabre parties. Some cult followers have since claimed that Credonia Mwerinde assembled them one day and reportedly said she was under instructions from the Virgin Mary to eat human flesh. She then requested them to pray hard so that they might be chosen for eating, since it would be an honour to allow oneself to be sacrificed in the name of the Madonna.

There have been claims that mothers were ordered to hand over their babies as a sacrifice to the Lord God. Hadn't the Lord ordered Abraham, their father in faith, to put the knife to his own son? Saddened by the request but yet terrified at the consequences of denying the Madonna's request, it is claimed that mothers handed over their children. It is said that Kaganga, the farm manager, was entrusted with the task of slaughtering babies. Each week Kibwetere and his apostles are reported to have feasted on a baby, a claim made by one ex-cultist during an interview with a local FM radio in Uganda soon after the inferno. This suggestion of sacrificing children is interesting in that while God ordered Abraham to sacrifice his son, once Abraham had shown he was willing to do so, God withdrew the order, accepting a ram instead. In fact the whole idea of a mother, especially the Holy Mother demanding such a sacrifice has got to be quite alien to anyone not completely mesmerised by this sort of cult.

Ex-cultists allege seeing Credonia, breath reeking of alcohol and hardly able to stand on her feet, with bloodstained lips and fresh crimson stains splashed on her white nun's dress. With glazed eyes and scowling face she looked like a vampire. One female ex-cultist reported that Credonia approached her with a request to sacrifice her baby in exchange for admission into the inner circle of the cult. Terrified, she made her escape from the cult compound that very evening.

It must be noted here that historically cannibalism or human sacrifice has never been associated with the mild and harmonious people of western Uganda. In fact, some of the ethnic groups in the region are strictly vegetarian and the closest they ever get to eat animal flesh is when they drink milk. Adherents of the Chwezi cult routinely slaughter sheep or goats as sacrifice to their deities and not humans. However, it is not entirely surprising when groups seeking to wield total control over their followers resort to cannibalism.

Cannibalism was a prominent feature on the battlefields of Liberia and Sierra Leone in the 1990s[50]. In these countries warring factions were in the business of brutally killing and eating members of rival militias. The liver and heart were much sought after (not for transplantation, you surmise). This was supposed to bestow upon the man-eater a mantle of invincibility and the prowess of a lion. Joseph Kibwetere and Dominic Kataribabo, being conversant with world events, must have been aware of this belief. Strange as it sounds Kibwetere and his apostles appear to have resorted to cannibalism as a means of gaining some kind of supernatural power and control over their followers. Evidently, as might be expected, the cult leadership had problems believing in their own divine faculty.

Besides eating and drinking, the inner circle organised sex orgies, conveniently overlooking the stern chastisements to befall violators of the Sixth and Ninth Commandments. An invitation to entertain heavenly visitors would be sent out to a select group of followers. When all were drunk the orgies would begin. With relentless libidos, like dogs on heat at full moon, the apostles pounced on their quarry. It was indiscriminate sex with total disregard to the dangers of AIDS. The old slept with the very young and same sex unions were a norm. It is widely believed that Father Dominic Kataribabo had a strong preference for sex with men and he is supposed to have surrounded himself with young men. He must have derived enormous pleasure from killing his sex partners judging from the skeletons found under the floor of his bedroom in Rugazi, where it has been alleged he organised regular sex orgies.

How could he have gone on killing for so long without being detected? Based on interviews with ex-cultists, some commentators of the bizarre cult cite the strict code of silence that ensured followers could not talk of their experiences. It is claimed that on mornings following the orgy, participants were summoned to appear before Kaganga. He would then promise death to anyone who dared share the activities of the previous evening with the uninitiated. Incredibly, he is reported to have insisted to the cultists that the orgies were just a small taste of greater things that awaited the faithful after the end of the present world. Some believed and stayed on. Others found the entire experience revolting and planned their escape. It is reported Kaganga thwarted quite a few escapes. The stories of these unfortunate would-be escapees lay buried in the banana plantation and pit latrines on the cult compound in Kanungu.

The routine of life in the camp was designed to ensure maximum docility. But such docility would last only as long as followers interpreted the teachings as valid and true. There were people who discovered numerous inconsistencies in cult doctrine or sensed that they were in company of false prophets. These people quit the organisation. Time is not static and followers were eagerly awaiting the end of this period and the beginning of a new order after the passing away of the current world.

When 29th December 1999 approached, an air of anticipation and apprehension hung over the cult compound. The chapel was scrubbed clean and decorated with bougainvillaea and hibiscus flowers, all done to welcome the dawning of a new age of eternity. It was a question of a few hours before the three days of darkness would assail the world. But nothing happened that day and not even during the course of the next day. The sun still rose in the east and set in the west.

Then cult leaders said the end would now happen on 31st December 1999 in spite of the visible absence of the all-important three days of darkness. Choosing the wisdom of their leaders over the certainty of cosmic laws, the faithful waited for the last trumpet that would herald the end.

When cultists awoke in the new millennium they were disappointed to discover nothing had really changed. The hills still occupied the same place and birds glided in the skies, just like every other day. Looking down the valley they could see locals going about their usual routines. It appeared the world was here to stay.

Feeling cheated and exploited, a group of angry cultists broke the rule of silence. They walked over to the leaders and demanded the end of the world there and then or else a refund of their money and return of other worldly assets. Credonia tried to calm them down. Not so fast, she said, claiming to have received an apparition the previous evening with a new message. The end of the world would happen between that moment and 31st December 2000.

Credonia's latest claim was reinforced by a vision supposedly revealed to Joseph Kibwetere and independent of her own apparition. Kibwetere sent a letter to the faithful reading, "I Joseph Kibwetere, my boss Jesus Christ, has appeared to me and handed me a message to all of you. It clarifies the issue of the world's end on 31 December 1999. This generation will now end before the end of the year 2000 after which no other year will follow." As usual a few sneered at the new message and walked back to their villages far poorer than when they had joined the ***Movement for the Restoration of the Ten Commandments of God***.

The more optimistic gave the cult leadership the benefit of the doubt and stayed on waiting for the end of the world. Some of the optimists had an infinite sense of compassion and saw a flash of hope in the time still available before the end of the world. They would utilise that period to minister to the sinful, particularly friends and relatives.

Not wishing to see his friends missing the redemption bandwagon, ex-police constable Deus Byamugisha, with full backing from the cult leadership, travelled to Kampala on a mission to convert and save former colleagues. While still actively serving on the force, he had shared great moments with his colleagues and Deus Byamugisha felt it would not only have been selfish but also irresponsible not to warn them of the coming end of the world. Saving even a single soul would be proof enough of not having reneged on his Christian obligation. It is thus that he headed for the police barracks in Kampala in a frantic effort to recruit ex-colleagues and their wives. Four policemen, close friends of his, did not require further prompting. They packed a few belongings and headed straight for Kanungu in the hope of escaping the fast approaching catastrophic three days of darkness.

Back at Kanungu Credonia Mwerinde and the other leaders were licking the wounds sustained following a public challenge to their doctrine and moral authority. With each day came new voices of dissent. A revolution, and perhaps a violent one, was in the making. Docility had given way to a fighting mood. Under increasing pressure from bold cultists demanding back their property and questioning the apparitions, religious fervour took on a strange twist. It is perhaps at this juncture that the cult leadership decided to muzzle the increasingly loud voices of dissent.

A brilliant plan was hatched, so it is now believed. Troublesome members would be secretly summoned for a rendezvous with the Blessed Virgin Mary at one of the four cult learning centres. It appears the cult leadership agreed on organising these gatherings at the centres in Rugazi, Rushojwa, Rukungiri and Buziga. The Buziga centre, located in a Kampala suburb, was the cult's first compound outside its stronghold of western Uganda. It had been in operation for one year and was considered to be of strategic financial importance. Buziga had been initially planned to serve as a launch pad into the deep pockets of the sons and daughters of western Ugandans living and working in Kampala and the enterprise of luring Kampala folk had been a resounding success. Quite a few natives of western Uganda living in and around Kampala were enrolled at the Buziga learning centre.

As for the remaining cult members the Madonna would reveal herself on 17th March 2000 inside the church building at the cult's main spiritual home in Kanungu. She would supposedly be in their presence through the three days of complete darkness from which they would emerge as a new generation. The new generation emerging in Year 1 would be unblemished by sin. The new people would then inherit the earth where they would live forever and ever.

Chapter 8
Last supper—a reconstruction

They will be like bits of straw, and a fire will burn them up! They will not even be able to save themselves—the flames will be too hot for them, not a cosy fire to warm themselves by. Isaiah 47:14

The precise chronology and the exact evolution of events that eventually culminated in what has come to be known as the Kanungu cult massacre remain a matter of educated speculation. Accounts given by ex-cultists and people residing in the immediate neighbourhood of cult compounds suggest that from around early January 2000 the main cult compound in Kanungu and the numerous learning centres began getting frequent nocturnal callers. Cultists could clearly see that these tough-looking, Swahili-speaking men were not of their kind. Unlike them, these men did not wear long flowing robes. Instead they dressed like heathen folk: dirty T-shirts and tattered trousers. If there were any cultists that suspected these men of evil intentions then the matter must not have been given much thought. Evildoers could not dare walk in the presence of the apostles in the manner that these men did, cultists must have reasoned. Cultists must have thought these men to be friends. If only they had known!

Some observers believe that these Swahili-speaking men ranked among the most violent murderers alive. For a few dollars they could be counted on to do a professional killing job. These were *interahamwe* hit men. On the run from justice for the genocide that they conducted, they now lived in the lawless parts of the Congo and Rwanda where civil government had totally collapsed. But those needing their services, like the leaders of the cult, must have known how to contact them. The *interahamwe* then proceeded to do the dirty work.

It is now believed that at the cult centres in Rushojwa, Buhunga and Rugazi, cultists were invited into a room to meet the Virgin Mary.

And most of those invited for a private chat with the Madonna were the very cult members that had made the most dissenting noises when the end of the world didn't happen on 31st December 1999 as prophesised by Kibwetere and his seers. Like lambs being led to the slaughter they walked into the room with great happiness and joy expecting to come face to face with a sweet smiling Madonna, the final reward for their total devotion. Instead, they encountered a team of unsmiling brutes blocking their path. Throats were slit open and the blood collected for the evening orgy or church ritual. In some cases, the brutes curled their powerful hands around the neck and with all their might, squeezed life out of their victims whose bewildered eyes popped out and mouths frothed, unable to let out a scream. The lifeless bodies were dumped in a pit dug for this very purpose.

But the *interahamwe* monsters were terrified of penetrating deep into the Uganda interior. They could not venture into Kampala, where the other cult compound was located. The Kampala branch, with its rather sophisticated membership, had to be dealt with differently. There, the ex-Catholic priest, Father Dominic Kataribabo, decided to wait until such a time that the leadership had dealt with its troublesome countryside following.

At the beginning of March 2000 Credonia Mwerinde and Joseph Kibwetere made the long awaited announcement. The Madonna had revealed to them that on Friday, 17th March 2000, the world would end. The faithful were urged to be at Kanungu on that important day in human history. Although the cult discouraged followers from listening to the radio and reading newspapers, as a means of keeping those residing permanently in the cult compound in perpetual ignorance, it began broadcasting messages on Voice of Toro, a local FM radio station, appealing to former cultists to return. At the same time the broadcasts attempted to recruit even more people into the group. Knowledge of the official end of the world swayed a few former cultists. One man sold his house for a pittance. All he wanted was just enough money to meet his bus fare to Kanungu. He assured the bewildered buyer that he wouldn't need any money in paradise. In haste, he caught the next bus to the cult's spiritual home in Kanungu.

Retracing the path that Father Dominic Kataribabo travelled in the dying days of the cult provides a fair idea of his possible role in the macabre events that would soon shock the world. After supervising *interahamwe* activity, in which he took immense pleasure, Father Dominic Kataribabo ordered his chauffeur to drive the pick-up truck northwards to the city of Kasese. Once in Kasese he instructed the driver to head for a motorcar garage, somewhere in the industrial area of the city. His chauffeur wondered what the purpose of this visit could be. But he was a mere mortal and never dared question a man who spoke directly to God.

Dressed in a black suit and wearing a white clerical collar, Dominic walked into the garage manager's office and inquired if it were possible to purchase forty litres of sulphuric acid. The manager dropped his jaw. He nearly shouted, "What the hell do you think you are going to do with so much acid? Burn the world or something?" But he checked his words just in time. One never showed disrespect to a rosary-clutching priest. Besides, what did it matter? As long as the man paid for the stuff he couldn't care less if the deranged cleric was determined to raze a couple of houses to the ground. Thus it was that the cult bought forty litres of sulphuric acid. The next stop was a petrol station where they bought sixty litres of paraffin.

There was just enough time to attend to the little matter of the Kampala branch members. So they headed off to the big city. When he got to the cult compound it was late in the evening. It had been a long journey on a rough road and the priest was feeling rather exhausted. The chauffeur received instructions not to park the car in the garage as was customary.

The fatigue left Father Kataribabo when he entered the cult house. It was fully packed. Quite a large number of Kampala-based members had taken the end of the world message seriously. Fifty-five people, mainly women and children, had gathered. After leading them through prayer he insisted on preparing and serving them tea. Most could not hear of it. Whoever heard of a leader of his standing serving mere mortals? But he quickly dismissed their protests arguing that even Jesus, in a show of humility, washed the feet of his disciples. So the issue was settled.

Later that afternoon he bumped into a troublesome Catholic bishop[51] . Once again the untiring bishop tried to lure him back to the Catholic Church. Kataribabo told him disparagingly that he could never join a Church that didn't communicate directly with God. Once again, the bishop's attempts at reaching out to this man ended in total defeat. That was on 15th March 2000. Kataribabo was running behind schedule, since he had to be in Kanungu the next day. The cult leadership had planned a "Last Supper" with their followers. He quickly supervised the Kampala activities. When all the evidence had been buried, it was time to head for Kanungu.

While Kataribabo was making his way back to Kanungu on that Thursday evening, Credonia Mwerinde and Joseph Kibwetere were presiding over a church service[52] . Chalices overflowing with blood were passed around. Followers partook in the miracle of wine turning into blood and counted themselves lucky for their foresight in teaming up with the seers.

When the service ended followers silently walked to the dining hall. For the entire day, men and women had been busy as bees preparing for this moment. It was the "Last Supper". After this meal there would be no more hunger. The definitive process that would see them through to paradise had already started. Over one thousand bottles of Coca-Cola had been brought in and three bulls slaughtered for the occasion. Credonia and Kibwetere had picked the bulls out personally. For the over five hundred people at the supper that day, it was the most fulfilling day of their life. It was also the first time that most cult members were eating a decent meal since abandoning their homes for the austerity of the cult compound. And the apostles were so generous, urging their followers not to be shy when it came to taking a second helping. The eating and drinking (all done in deadly silence) went on deep into the night.

Just before the cultists retired to their dormitories, one young lad, who had left the party to attend to a call of nature, caught sight of two people hurriedly heading for the banana plantations. He thought the two shadowy figures, bags tucked under their arms, belonged to Credonia Mwerinde and Joseph Kibwetere[53] . When he got back to the dining room it was time for night prayers. The prayers were led by one of the apostles. Many could not sleep that night as images of wondrous times ahead drifted through their imagination.

Cultists awoke to a beautiful morning. The sky was deep blue and the sun hovered above the hills in the east. Brightly coloured birds fluttered and chirped. Roosters crowed and cows mooed. In the distance, somewhere in Kanungu trading centre, cultists heard the sound of a minibus engine, just like on most mornings. It backfired a couple of times before squeaking up the winding hilly path that led out of Kanungu. Everything seemed so normal. The morning of 17th March 2000 looked just like the morning of the day before and the morning of any other day. In other words, it seemed to be the kind of morning that one could not easily associate with the end of the world. But to cultists this spelled the end of this generation and the beginning of three days of darkness. Breakfast was not served that morning because they had eaten their last earthly meal the previous night. A few yawns could be seen here and there. Then the gong summoning cultists to gather in "the ark" was sounded. It was time to go to the chapel and wait for the passing of the three days of darkness. In single file they headed for the chapel.

Going through the list of those that perished on that day we can attempt to reconstruct what might have taken place that morning on the Kanungu cult compound.

A 43-year old mother of five led her four children into the chapel. But behind her exterior shell of joy she was in a state of deep pain. Her fifth child, a lad of seventeen, had failed to make it to Kanungu. If only he had acted urgently he would have counted himself among the redeemed.

One man could not help thinking about his ex-wives. He had been in a polygamous marriage and once had three wives. Because the cult didn't permit followers to have more than one wife, he had abandoned two of them. It hadn't been easy separating from them. Clan elders were called to arbitrate. "A man's wealth is counted by the number of wives he is able to keep in his homestead," the elders had said. But when he countered arguing that polygamy barred entry into the Lord God's Kingdom, the elders pronounced him crazy. With his favourite wife, his latest acquisition, a most attractive young woman of nineteen, he had joined the cult. He might have gone on reminiscing about his ex-wives if he hadn't caught a glimpse of the glowing face of his beloved. At that moment he must have wished it were possible to hold her in his arms. But he knew the commandments and instead just smiled back at his lovely wife.

Eight men, all from the same village, could not believe their luck as they marched to the chapel escaping the tribulations that would soon be unleashed upon a disobedient world.

A woman, carrying her two-year-old twins, was having trouble keeping them quiet. She stepped out of the queue, saw a tree, and headed for its shade. Just as she was about to give the hungry twins the breast, Kaganga wagged a disapproving finger. She abandoned the effort lest she missed entering "the ark".

One of the apostles huddled a group of playing children into the chapel. In the process, he nearly knocked down a pregnant woman just making her entry into the building.

Seventeen-year-old Ahimbisibwe could not contain the hunger pangs assailing him. If he was going to paradise it had better be with a full stomach, he reasoned. He made a dash for his father's home, some couple of kilometres outside the cult compound, in the hope of hurriedly eating some bananas. If his calculations were right he would just be in time to get into the chapel.

With Christian valour and humility, the followers of the ***Movement for Restoration of the Ten Commandments*** marched into the chapel. Neatly shaved heads, clean flowing robes and huge rosaries dangling from their necks, they were all set for the three days of universal darkness. "What were three days of total darkness to man?" they must have queried. The chapel windows and doors were tightly bolted. Not even a mouse could escape. With daylight curtained off and no shafts of light entering the chapel, darkness was complete inside the chapel. There were over five hundred of them—men, women and children—hoping to encounter the Virgin Mary in the palpable obscuration of "the ark".

At about midday while the cultists were singing hymns in their chapel, Didas Rwemiyaga was doing a spot of gardening a few hundred meters down the road. He had to clear the weeds from his coffee garden just before the rains. It was scorching hot under the sun. Beads of sweat ran freely down his forehead, and onto his cheeks and chin. Feeling thirsty, he turned to walk over to his calabash of *obushera*[54] . Before he could get to the calabash there was a deafening explosion. Didas froze in his tracks and tightened his grip on the hoe. His first reaction was one of flight. He thought the *interahamwe* had attacked.

The previous year, around the same time, the *interahamwe* had abducted a group of western tourists who were out in the mountains tracking gorillas[55] . Uganda government soldiers had given hot pursuit. Machine-gun fire and heavy artillery could be heard in Kanungu as troops took on the thugs. Could it be that the slayers had now attacked Kanungu? But when he looked in the direction of the explosion he quickly dismissed the thought.

A huge fire had engulfed one of the buildings in the cult compound, and the flames appeared to be roaring out of control and there were agonising cries for help. It is then that it dawned on Didas that there were people trapped in the burning building.

Didas ran to the cult's compound as fast as his legs could carry him. But he arrived too late. And so were the other rescuers from Kanungu. With no fire extinguishers all they could do was watch on helplessly as the fire fiercely raged on hushing the cries of those trapped in the chapel. Didas had never imagined the sheer devastating force of fire as he watched the last of what had been left of the tin roof burn away as if it were a stack of dry hay.

It was then that he heard a muffled scream rise above the crackling sound of the flames. It was the unmistakable cry of an infant in distress. He remembered his own child back home. Heart-broken and anguished, he rushed to the crumbling chapel, but the unbearable heat radiating from the unrelenting fire put a stop to his valiant performance. One man filled a mug with water and urged the others to do the same. Four other villagers thought it a fantastic idea, and with less than three litres of water between them, frantically tried to douse the conflagration. Others crossed themselves several times over and prayed for divine intervention. Most, however, screamed and yelled, as if that alone could somehow tame the roaring fire forcing it to die down.

That afternoon, when the fire had run its course, it seemed as if the entire population of Kanungu and surrounding hamlets had gathered at the cult's compound. Nobody had ever seen a tragedy like this.

Its magnitude and sheer cruelty was unparalleled in the recent and past history of this sleepy village nestling in lush hills of astounding beauty.

Charred bodies lay in all sorts of contorted positions and piled on top of each other. Some of the charred remains were in postures that suggested a possible struggle to climb the chapel walls and get out to safety. Most of the bodies were burnt beyond recognition, but the one lying close to the door was in reasonable shape. It was evidently a huge man. His skin was a mass of badly burned flesh and there was a white clerical collar around his neck. He held a doorknob in his hand and there was a baby in the crook of his other arm held tightly to his chest. Some villagers swore that this was Father Dominic Kataribabo.

Those in the crowd who fancied themselves as detectives began speculating about the significance of this latest observation. Apparently, they argued, the plan was to have Father Kataribabo entertain the cultists with a good sermon while one of his accomplices set fire onto the chapel. As soon as the fire was going the accomplice was supposed to have opened the door and together they would make their escape. However, with the whole place overwhelmed by the fire and babies screaming for a chance to live, even the hardened Father Kataribabo was moved. He must have tried to save just one baby, which he held in his arms as he dashed for the door. But his accomplice had fled out of the smoke-filled furnace and bolted the door firmly behind him.

Other villagers dismissed the theory. They argued that the cult leaders were incapable of showing compassion and most likely weren't caught up in the fire. They were certain Credonia Mwerinde and Joseph Kibwetere must have escaped.

It was a gruesome scene. Tears flowed freely and people asked themselves how such a thing could ever be allowed to happen in their quiet corner of the world. How many had been killed? Again, villagers were undecided. Someone shouted that the number was over ten thousand. Another villager had taken the trouble to count, and he thought the number was more like two hundred. Clearly the task of counting and identifying the dead was far beyond them. The local government representative rang his bosses in Kampala and delivered the grim news. A shattered President Museveni expressed shock at the "horrific, senseless and tragic" incident.

Down at Kanungu prison a middle-aged man was serving a one-year prison term for tax defaulting; he had failed to pay the annual graduated tax levelled on every adult male in Uganda. Like most inmates he had heard the explosion. News had spread equally fast and prisoners knew that a group of religious zealots had burnt to death. However, little did the man and his fellow inmates suspect that they would shortly be involved with this gruesome event.

On Sunday, they were ordered to march, single-file, to the cult compound. Prison warders, Kalashnikov rifles held at the ready, made sure none of the prisoners tried to retreat. Some prisoners carried hoes and others had shovels. Most of them just walked along empty-handed. The stench of putrid human flesh assailed their nostrils and seemed to diffuse through their entire being.

When they arrived at the devastated compound, a mass of decomposing charred bodies covered by countless flies stared right back at them. Even the hardened criminals among them could not stomach the scene. One man started retching but the unimpressed guard ordered him on mercilessly. The prisoners were ordered to dig deep ditches a few metres from the razed church. Onlookers held rosemary sprigs to their nostrils to fend off the overpowering stench of death.

The bereaved relatives mourned and screamed at this senseless tragedy. One woman, totally deranged by the magnitude of her loss, pleaded with the policemen guarding the site to allow her get to her husband and three sons. She insisted they had to be alive somewhere under the burnt rubble. An elderly man fainted on seeing the amorphous tangle of rotting bodies. His grandchildren had perished in the inferno. A dog had succeeded in pulling off an arm from a body and was quietly chewing his dinner. In an attempt to force the dog abandon its human meal, a villager scooped a mound of red earth and hurled it at the man-eater. The dog snarled angrily at him but made no effort to abandon its free lunch. With the arm in its mouth, the dog just moved to a quieter corner of the compound.

With shovels, hoes and bare-hands, prisoners shoved the bodies into the mass graves. Bare-foot, wearing the standard prison garb of white khaki shirts and short trousers, the prisoners laboured the entire day. It was a task they were ill equipped to perform. The next day a bulldozer arrived to ease their task. It levelled off what remained of the church wall, scooped the rotting bodies and dumped them into the trenches. An inmate engaged in the business of clearing up the mess acknowledged it was the most difficult assignment he had ever been required to undertake. "I couldn't eat for sometime because my hands still smelled of the stench," this man said.

According to him, inmates involved in burying the cultists were never given water to bathe after the exercise. A leading Ugandan psychiatrist would condemn the barbaric way in which prisoners had been treated. Human rights organisations were not pleased. It was inhuman for the police to use prisoners without protective clothing and proper equipment to bury the dead[56] . Even a senior prison officer found the deployment of prisoners for the exercise deplorable. The officer said, "It is definitely inhuman to expose prisoners to danger. When you assist someone with first aid you should not become the next casualty."

When the bulldozer piled the last of the red earth on the mass graves, one of the onlookers made a poignant observation, "These people died in the process of searching for the ultimate Christian prize. Today, they are being buried without anyone uttering a Christian prayer for them. Where are the Church leaders?"

To believe that all onlookers at the solemn burial ceremony were grieving families or people assembled because of a sense of deep loss is to draw wrong conclusions about human nature. Some folks, practised in the art of exploiting golden opportunities, arrived on the scene crying louder than the bereaved. They quickly took in the entire scene and saw an opportunity where many would be at a loss to find one. Realising that it was impossible, save for a miracle, for cult leaders to return and reclaim property on the compound, these folks took it upon themselves to raid the place. This heralded the arrival of looters.

Cows and chickens were whisked away. One man was seen carrying away three statues of the Virgin Mary that he had managed to remove from the cult's main office. Another man raided the cult storerooms and happily walked out with a neat pile of green and black robes. When asked why he had chosen the cult uniforms instead of the plastic cups and plates that seemed to have an obvious practical use, he smiled sheepishly and muttered something about using the garments as substitute for blankets.

Then a bizarre rumour began circulating. It was whispered that the cult had lots of money buried somewhere on the compound. But nobody seemed to know the exact location of the treasure. Under cover of darkness fortune hunters descended on the compound. They carried hoes and shovels and sticks. One group started their treasure hunt in the vegetable garden, a couple of metres away from the mass grave. Instead of coming up with a casket of money their shovels unearthed decomposing human bodies. Another man had convinced himself that the casket of money had to be somewhere in the hole of the pit latrine. He shone a torch down the dark pit anticipating scooping out clean crispy dollar notes. But his loud scream, waking up half of Kanungu, was not a shout of triumph at the retrieval of treasure. Five bodies had been dumped in the pit. It is these activities, and not some fancy detective work, that alerted the police to a possibility of other dead cultists buried on cult property.

In the coming days a nation gripped in shock and fear witnessed the uncovering of more horror as police searched numerous cult properties. Two mass graves, containing a total of one hundred and fifty-three bodies, were found at Buhunga, a cult centre that was a couple of kilometres from Kanungu. At Father Dominic Kataribabo's house in Rugazi, seventy-three bodies were dug up from a mass grave in his sugar plantation. Beneath the floor of his bedroom, eighty-one bodies were exhumed. At Rushojwa, another cult learning centre, over eighty bodies were recovered from a mass grave in the banana garden. In all these instances, the single police pathologist working on the case established that most of the victims had been strangled or stabbed to death. And in a Kampala suburb residents alerted police of a foul odour coming from a house known to belong to the cult. There, in the garage of the house, police found fifty-five bodies that had been hurriedly dumped into a shallow grave.

The pathologist suspected that the Kampala cultists had been poisoned. The ***Movement for the Restoration of the Ten Commandments of God*** had murdered over one thousand of its followers. The toll was far in excess of the 1978 Jonestown tragedy in which nine hundred and thirteen people—largely members of the Californian Peoples Temple—were killed after poisoning with a cyanide-laced drink. But why, once exposed for the charlatans they were, did the leaders of the cult choose murdering their followers over fleeing the country?

To understand this question one needs to look at the deep-rooted cynicism exhibited by most people outside of Africa when it comes to condemning or acting against mass murder in Africa. It would appear that there is no government either in or outside the continent that loses sleep over reports of slaughtered Africans. The killing of elephants or gorillas is more likely to generate deeper sympathy from the affluent civilised world. For people living in western Uganda and sharing a common border with Rwanda, events in the latter country are living testimony to this.

Rwanda desensitised people to the value of human life because of the ease with which hundreds of thousands of people were killed before any significant noises of disapproval were made. Also in the unlikely event that a vicious murderous regime is overthrown, the perpetrators of the heinous crimes can always flee to safety in the civilised world. Once there these leaders are most likely to be rewarded for their evil deeds. And the reward package is hefty, often including a mansion and twenty-four hour police protection.

Consider a few examples to illustrate this point. Idi Amin, the monstrous butcher of Uganda, presided over the slaughter of half a million Ugandans during an eight-year reign of terror. No serious attempts were ever made by the international community to drag him before an international court to answer for his gruesome deeds. He lived as a free man somewhere on the Arabian Peninsula.[57]

When the architects of the 1994 Rwanda genocide turned up in some western capitals they were received with open arms as if they were Roman generals returning after a successful military campaign against some savages in the dark heartland of Africa. Kibwetere and other cult leaders were not oblivious to these facts. They could burn and hack followers to death in the full knowledge that nobody would bother bringing them to face justice for their atrocities.

Chapter 9
Looking the other way

It so happened that a priest was going down that road; but when he saw the man, he walked on by, on the other side. Luke 10:31

Most disturbing to a grieving nation was the fact that the killings happened in an area known to be a stronghold of the ruling NRM of President Yoweri Museveni; and that among those murdered, women and children were over-represented. Even going by the standards of a nation with an unfortunate propensity for being subjected to terror, this event was too much to bear. A young female lawyer calling a talk show program on a Kampala FM radio station lamented, "If the government could not protect the lives of its most staunch supporters from capricious opportunists then who is really safe? I am scared to walk in the street." Why then, did the government ignore the activities of this cult?

Some junior officials had in fact kept a tab on the activities of the cult. They were not entirely pleased with what they saw. For example, these officials strongly suspected the Kibwetere group of deliberately killing children. People had complained about relatives who went to join the cult but were never to be seen again. On more than one occasion these officials appealed to their superiors to take action against the cult. But nothing was done.

Just before the cult embarked on systematic murder of its followers, one woman, Ms Mitima, had suspected that her mother, a cult member, had died under mysterious circumstances while in one of the cult compounds where she had gone to seek spiritual enlightenment[58]. She had reason to believe that her mother's death was not due to hypertension as the cult claimed. She strongly suspected foul play. Attempts to bring her suspicions to the attention of different security organs encountered an amazing degree of stonewalling. At the police station the constables listened to her story with utmost sympathy and scribbled furiously in their notepads. But for months no action was taken. The mysterious death of an ageing woman was hardly the kind of thing that security agents considered a serious breach of law and order hence warranting a closer look. They therefore ignored the crying woman.

Interestingly, suspicions of the cult's darker side were not confined to only a few people. Disturbing as it may be, people living in the neighbourhood of the learning centres had long suspected the cult of engaging in sex orgies and human sacrifices. A couple of villagers claim to have known that the cult reserved Friday mornings for the ritual slaughter of children, an allegation that also appeared in the government controlled media[59] . Because of a deep sense of fear none felt courageous enough to report the matter to law and order enforcement agencies or even to civil authorities. This culture of silence is a hangover from the Idi Amin era of terror.

Most Ugandans were aware of Idi Amin's torture chambers operated by the Gestapo-like State Research Bureau (SRB) where thousands were brought to a brutal death. But none dared to speak out because of fear that they might become the SRB's next victims. It was only after Idi Amin's overthrow that people felt confident enough to openly discuss their fears. Therefore, it is not surprising that villagers found it easier to talk about the evil side of Kibwetere's religious movement in hushed voices.

They might not have belonged to the cult but villagers believed the cult leaders to be people endowed with mystical qualities. Credonia Mwerinde's supposed expertise in the black art of witchcraft was a recognised, albeit feared, phenomenon—at least in Kanungu and its immediate environs. One woman said that Credonia only needed to look at someone through squinted eyes to cause discord in one's marital life. She added, "All of a sudden you begin noticing that your spouse has halitosis and stinking feet, as if he has been cleaning the public latrine with bare feet." To protect herself from the Credonia spell, this woman said she had learned not to stare back at Credonia. Her precautionary stance must have worked because she still had her husband.

These factors were enough to frighten villagers suspecting foul play, out of their wits. Most villagers might have doubted that the police would believe the tales of simple peasants implicating powerful intellectuals of the stature of Father Dominic Kataribabo in satanic activities. And anyway, the villagers did not have solid evidence. So what factors could explain the government's attitude of turning a deaf ear to potentially dangerous cult activities? Numerous reasons have been advanced.

The government and the ***Movement for the Restoration of the Ten Commandments of God*** pursued a common agenda on numerous fronts. In the beginning, the cult requested its members to be obedient to government officials. This went down quite well with secular authorities. Of course, a group preaching righteous living was not the kind that any government could perceive as a security threat—at least, on the surface. If somebody was urging citizens not to rob, kill and commit adultery it meant less crime and a much better community. Warning of the dangers of AIDS was seen as an enormous contribution to public health. These values were complementary to government efforts aimed at creating peaceful, healthy and law-abiding citizens. This was all the better for increased productivity and taxation.

But perhaps most important to government was the cult's position in fighting what the Kibwetere group referred to as "sexual perversion". Waging total war against sexual perversion was also a matter very dear to Mr. Museveni and a few like-minded African presidents like Mr. Robert Mugabe of Zimbabwe.[60] The cult ranted against homosexuality and so did Mr. Museveni and his government. Uganda law states that "carnal knowledge of another against the order of nature" will be punished by a possible life sentence. This is an archaic piece of legislature inherited from the British at independence but still jealously and fervently guarded by self-proclaimed moral puritans. The Ugandan president, Mr. Museveni, had this to say about same-sex relationships, "I have told the Criminal Investigation Department to look for homosexuals, lock them up and charge them. The Bible spells it out clearly that God created Adam and Eve. I did not see God creating man and man."[61]

The president's anti-homosexual crusade, in his opinion inspired by the Bible, appealed to a certain small but vocal core of ruling party extremists. Notable among them was a self-righteous Mr. Kakooza, a Kampala journalist, profiling himself as the custodian of morality in the country. He claimed that the president had supported his efforts to form a vigilante group whose aim was best summarised in his own words, "We're working against these immoral fellows who are duping the public that they are exercising human rights. What rights does one man have when it comes to having carnal knowledge of his fellow man?" Therefore, it is evident that some aspects of cult philosophy could not be disentangled from ruling party policy. In the matter of persecuting homosexuals the government viewed the cult as a worthy partner in stopping what it considered as moral decay in the country.

Both the cult leaders and the ruling elite in Uganda hailed from the western parts of the country. This is a very pertinent point to make. Western Uganda was, therefore, a natural constituency of the government. In the unlikely event of an election, the ruling party could always count on the region to overwhelm its political opponents. According to some reports, cultists voted overwhelmingly for candidates who were endorsed by the ruling NRM party[62] . On the basis of this narrow sectarian assumption, the government considered western Uganda as an area posing no threat to its hold on power.

Because it was taken for granted that no political agitators could flourish in the region, the presence of police or other security agents was at its thinnest in the Kanungu area. Besides, coming from the western region helped cult leaders build a network of friends with connections reaching the uppermost rung of the political ladder. Cult leaders even claimed to have met Mr. Museveni at his palatial countryside home in Rwakitura and handed him a copy of their paperbound spiritual booklet[63] .

When the pope visited Uganda, Kibwetere and a number of his apostles are said to have managed to shake hands with him. Some suspect that his friends in high places arranged this. However, after the Kanungu inferno the pope's representative rejected these allegations, stating emphatically that "people don't meet the pope just like that."[64] This is probably true when the people referred to by the papal nuncio are ordinary Ugandan peasants. Truth is that Kibwetere had long since ceased belonging to the ordinary people of Uganda.

The cult was a successful business enterprise with plenty of money to grease the palms of many a corrupt official occupying positions of influence. Money donations to the right friends could open doors for cult leaders. And the cult was master at buying the co-operation of these political heavyweights. It was not unusual for politicians to visit the main cult compound in Kanungu. Paying such a visit was a worthwhile enterprise that assured the politician of numerous gifts. Cows were donated to favoured politicians and trays of eggs were loaded into shiny official limousines. Starving children and famished women in flowing black robes would be ordered by the apostles to go into the fields and gather the very best vegetables and fruits for the eating pleasure of the politician's family. The concerned politician, bulging belly and satisfied smile, would shower praise on Kibwetere and his group for running such an exemplary law-abiding community. One politician had such a close relationship with the group that female cultists were sent down to his house on numerous occasions to cook his meals and who knows what other things.

Strong political connections and the use of bribery enabled the cult to go on with its dangerous activities without fear of being investigated. Police came knocking quite a few times at the cult's Kanungu headquarters in an attempt to investigate allegations of killing children. But someone made sure their reports never made it to the regional police headquarters. Those that were too nosy would be rewarded with a transfer to some remote, out-of-the-way place.

The cult tried to embrace people of all faiths, a philosophy that appeared to work. Among the dead were a couple of Muslims who had been lured away from their faith. Protestants of all denominations were also recruited. However, in the main, the rank and file of the cult were predominately ex-Catholics. To understand the relevance of this factor in explaining the government's inaction it is pertinent at this point to digress.

One of the first priorities of the ruling NRM government on attaining power in 1986 was to move speedily in the matter of ensuring that the activities of other political parties were suspended. It established something that it referred to as a "no party" movement, which is in effect just another name for a one party state. Every Ugandan, voluntarily or otherwise, supposedly belonged to this political movement. Persons aspiring for high political office, according to this newfangled and curious ideology, are elected on individual merit and not because of any affiliation to a particular political organisation. Party politics was at best divisive and at worst non-African, so argued the proponents of this system.

A referendum held in 2000 appeared to have resulted in overwhelming support for the one party system as the preferred permanent form of government. Subsequently, all other political parties were banned and the NRM was presumably to guide Ugandans for many generations to come. However, not many were convinced[65]. Political commentators have pointed out that the ruling NRM government was in awe of the predominantly Catholic Democratic Party (DP), which, although banned, remained a credible form of opposition with enormous potential for defeating the NRM in a fair democratic race.

Perennial opportunists or outright murderers provide leadership of the other political parties opposed to the NRM—hardly the required credentials to endear the electorate to these parties. Therefore, anything that weakened the Democratic Party's organisational structure or dented its Catholic constituency was apt to be greeted with glee. When Kibwetere and his apostles began recruiting among Catholics, NRM die-hards looked at it as a way of eroding the Democratic Party's political base. These ex-Catholics, nurtured by Kibwetere on a doctrine hostile to the Church that initially baptised them, could not be expected to support the DP. As long as Kibwetere targeted Catholics nobody in government was particularly bothered, since his success translated into weakening the DP and swelling the ruling party ranks as cultists were likely to show support on basis of tribal sentiment.

Because of its engagement in numerous wars, both internal and external, the government stretched its security forces too thin. The consequence of this was a breakdown in law and order within the country. In both the north and parts of western Uganda, the government was tied down having to deal with guerrillas bent on the violent overthrow of the ruling NRM of Mr. Museveni[66]. As if this were not enough on its plate, Mr. Museveni together with his Rwandan allies invaded the Democratic Republic of the Congo.

Apart from NRM die-hards it is hard to find sympathy among Ugandans for a senseless war that cost the lives of thousands of young Ugandan men in their prime, not to mention poisoning the once cordial relationship between the two peoples[67] . The war in the Congo that brought numerous African armies to confront and slay each other is yet another sad reminder of that unique propensity of African leaders to sacrifice the hopes and aspirations of their people by blindly and selfishly pursuing short-term policies of personal enrichment.

With more important things like fighting the war in the Congo preoccupying its mind, the government hardly had the time or the manpower to provide enough security for its citizens within the country's boundaries. Besides, the Uganda police force was understaffed, poorly trained and ill equipped. At the height of cult killings, the police force totalled only fifteen thousand men and women.

Even in the rare cases where police constables were still capable of smart detective work, corruption in the force ensured that their efforts were thwarted. Some government officials habitually obstructed police work. The police would definitely feel disobliged to conduct a thorough investigation if a ruling party apparatchik (or their friends) happened to be involved in suspicious activity. Attempts by a few spirited officers to investigate the cult attest to obstruction of legal proceedings of law and order. With their good connections to ruling party officials, the door was wide open for Kibwetere and his apostles to conduct any form of mischief with little fear from security agents.

Back now to the ***Movement***. What is in a name? some might be tempted to muse. In choosing a name for the cult, Kibwetere and his apostles were not only trying to send an unambiguous message to potential followers about their doctrine, but they also aimed at soothing the often unpredictable moods of ruling party officials.

Kibwetere called his organisation the "***Movement for the Restoration of the Ten Commandments of God***". This name presented no problems to the government. There was no explicit or implicit threat inherent in it. Instead, the name bore a close similarity to that of the ruling party—the National Resistance Movement

(NRM). It is important to emphasise the fact that both groups operated institutions that were known as movements. Interestingly, both the Kibwetere group and the NRM claimed to be umbrella organisations. The secular NRM claimed to incorporate everybody irrespective of prior political affiliation. The Kibwetere spiritual movement made an identical claim—it welcomed everybody irrespective of prior religious affiliation.

The NRM came onto the Uganda political scene with an ambitious Maoist political agenda known as the ten-point program. Kibwetere and his apostles had the Ten Commandments. The NRM runs special schools in which cadres are taught its political ideology. Often people are forced to attend these courses. In some cases promotion in the civil service or being awarded a government contract is dependent on proof of attendance at these courses. The ***Movement for the Restoration of the Ten Commandments of God*** ran learning centres to teach its spiritual ideology. People weren't forced into the centres, but once there, it was not easy to find their way out. Good scores on the attendance scale were rewarded.

Kibwetere and his apostles claimed to have monopoly over a spiritual vision that would lead sinners to an eternal life of happiness, and top NRM leaders often boasted of being the custodians of an almost divinely inspired political vision that would guide the poor peasantry in Uganda, transforming the country into a rich industrialised society[68]. And the similarities between these two movements are numerous. By choosing to borrow terminology and organisational style from the ruling party, the cult cultivated an image that was acceptable to government.

Disinclination to act in face of evidence incriminating the cult in abuse of human rights exposes the thick-skinned attitude adopted not only by the Uganda ruling elite, but also many other leaders in Africa, when it comes to dealing with issues that concern the well being of citizens. Civil authorities in Africa show interest in the people as long as they continue growing crops that bring the much-needed cash into state coffers to purchase military hardware. Charles Onyango-Obbo, Uganda's celebrated award-winning journalist and political commentator, noted that questioning the government about its shameful failure to act against the cult was to give undue credit to an African government[69].

Onyango-Obbo made this observation not because his liberal and objective opinions would make it hard for him to extol the dismal achievements of African dictatorships but rather to underscore the imprudent nature of political leadership in Africa. He was most probably speaking for the silent majority in the country. African governments are just not interested in their people. As long as no noises are made to challenge the ruling elite's monopoly on power, cultists or other opportunists are free to walk into any African country of their choice and subject its people to the most inhuman form of treatment without running the risk of ever being apprehended. They can therefore humiliate, abduct, torture, maim and kill. The golden rule is not to challenge the political leadership. Joseph Kibwetere and his apostles were fully aware of this.

Chapter 10
Inferno aftermath

You will hear the cries of the oppressed and the orphans; you will judge in their favour, so that mortal men may cause terror no more. Psalm 10:18

In the immediate aftermath of the Kanungu inferno the government, much to its credit, conducted business in a very honourable manner. It refrained from pandering to the rhetoric of those calling for harsher treatment of fringe religious groups. And quite a few people were demanding a total ban on these churches. "If I had the power, I would outlaw these cults and sects and leave only the mainstream Christian Churches and Muslims," a bitter parliamentarian representing Kanungu declared. He also wanted Mr. Museveni's wife to show leadership by denouncing her membership of her Pentecostal congregation and return to the mainstream Protestant Church.

Some argued that the Kanungu episode had nothing to do with mainstream versus fringe Christian groups. The most important thing to learn from the tragedy, these people said, was that it was high time to revise the Bible. None expounded this argument more eloquently than the director of a Uganda-based group calling itself the Independent Bible Scholars.

The director blamed the Bible for inspiring the cult to rob followers of their belongings and eventually to kill them. To support his argument he turned to the Bible and provided a rather long list of verses that seemed to legitimise the evil deeds of Kibwetere[70]. And according to this independent scholar of the Bible, the government ought to provide leadership by excluding from Holy Scriptures texts that seem to convey an impression that evil campaigns are perfectly legitimate. Instead of passing some draconian law or attempting to re-write the Christian Holy Scriptures, the government preferred a more sane and humane approach.

Plans to appoint a six-member team led by a high court judge to probe the cult were announced. The judicial commission of inquiry would also be charged with suggesting recommendations regarding the degree of freedom that the government should grant the mushrooming religious sects. In the meantime the murdered victims would be mourned in a decent manner.

Accordingly, a national day of prayer was announced and set for 2nd April 2000. Prayers were held on the main cult compound in Kanungu. On that day the few proud owners of the national flag, such as the prison in Kanungu, flew the black, yellow and red national symbol of identity at half-mast. It was in respect to the dead, prison officials said.

An impressive delegation whose members came all the way from Kampala, attended the ceremony. Glittering four-wheel drive cars with shrilling sirens and travelling at speeds usually associated with the Paris-Dakar rally filled the normally car-shy road leading to Kanungu. All were headed for the day of national mourning. No villager could remember such an impressive collection of cars.

And their occupants were no ordinary Ugandans either. There was Uganda's vice president, Mrs. Specioza Kazibwe[71] , in a black mourning suit and wearing designer sunglasses accompanied by several ministers and numerous ruling party heavyweights.

A keen observer of the Uganda political scene could not help noting the irony. Hounded by accusations of financial misconduct, Mrs. Kazibwe had sought to prove her innocence by invoking the Virgin Mary's name. She made it known to the committee of legislators investigating her alleged financial impropriety that she was the Virgin's daughter and therefore above sleaze[72]. The committee seemed to be contented with her divine connections since it never probed the matter any further.

Another curious observation is that in April 1999, Uganda's vice president had played hostess to Dr. Hak Ja Han Moon, wife of the leader of the Unification Church, regarded by some in Uganda as a controversial cult. In spite of much protest from both inside and outside of the country, the vice president had then invited about four thousand ruling party faithful to attend a lecture on what was termed "social development and spiritualism" given by Dr. Hak Ja Han Moon. The image of an over-enthusiastic vice president eager to please her guest led one renowned scholar, Professor Timothy Wangusa, to pose a pertinent question, “What was a self-professed devout Roman Catholic signifying by consorting with a cult that is at odds with the teachings of mainstream Christianity?”

But at Kanungu these embarrassing little issues seemed to have been forgotten. The government’s immediate concern was to show some form of solidarity with the grieving families. In the words of one government minister it was time to “console surviving relatives and assure the country that action is being taken in pursuit of the criminal perpetrators of this evil.” It was a worthwhile gesture albeit one that came too late. And many grieving families shared this sentiment.

Addressing the mourners Mrs. Kazibwe described Kibwetere and his friends as “diabolic, malevolent criminals masquerading as holy and religious people”—a classic case of a good apple rotten at the heart. She admitted government had been lax in preventing the massacres and apologised for its shortcomings. This apology should be applauded. It is not everyday that an African government admits to conducting state affairs in a sloppy and insensitive manner. But then, Uganda’s vice president stood out as someone who abhorred mincing words. Whereas her male cabinet colleagues tried to steer clear of the smell of death by putting as much distance as possible between themselves and the burnt chapel, Kazibwe displayed no such cowardice. She walked amidst the broken statues and countless half-burnt rosaries scattered in the ruins of the chapel, shaking hands and consoling the bereaved families.

During the open-air interdenominational prayers for the murdered victims, Catholic, Protestant, Greek Orthodox, and Muslim clerics said a prayer for the dead. Compassionate and courageous words came from the Reverend Grace Kaiso of the Uganda Joint Christian Council, “As we stand at this disgraced place of Kanungu, we are forced to face our own failure in duty towards our neighbour. We failed in our duty and return to ask forgiveness.”

As floral wreaths were laid on the red earth of the mass graves, a choir of local Kanungu children sang. Innocent children sang hymns for playmates lured or forcefully dragged to their death. Their beautiful tender voices laden with melancholy floated over the assembled mourners before settling down into the valley. It was youthful music quivering with fear and then working towards a fast moving crescendo that gave hope to a broken nation.

Tear-filled eyes were not confined just to the gathered villagers. A few dignitaries were seen wiping away a tear or two. Among the mourners was Theresa Kibwetere. Just before the fire that engulfed the movement's chapel, she had received a letter from her estranged husband in which he urged her to continue with his ministry because the group was going to perish. Although there were fears that families of cult victims might take the law in their hands and lynch Mrs. Kibwetere, it is commendable that such a thing did not happen. Reason and restraint prevailed. Villagers were aware that Mrs. Kibwetere and her children had rejected the cult long ago. People understood that it was wrong to punish a wife for the wrongs of a roguish husband let alone penalising children for the evil deeds of their parents.

As might have been expected most folks tried to distance themselves as much as possible from Kibwetere and his cult. Overnight, the ***Movement for the Restoration of the Ten Commandments of God*** had acquired the status of a national pariah. The names Joseph Kibwetere, Credonia Mwerinde and Dominic Kataribabo came to symbolise the very incarnation of evil. Even close friends of the cult who through the years had given the movement spiritual inspiration, began to deny any links with it. An Australian seer, "the little pebble", who had visited the Movement on at least two occasions, was vehement in his denial of ever having met the Ugandan cult leader or any other member of the group. He claimed he wouldn't know Joseph Kibwetere "from a bar of soap."

There were even efforts, albeit incredulous, to portray Kibwetere and his followers as non-Ugandans. This school of deniers argued that Ugandans are incapable of the kind of barbarism displayed by the cult leadership and that the people of Uganda are too smart to fall prey to the likes of Kibwetere. A leading lawyer hailing from Kibwetere's home region wrote a long treatise in one of the Uganda newspapers claiming that the name Kibwetere was not native to the area. The foreign nature of the name, the lawyer argued, strongly suggested that the cult leader probably had his origins in the Democratic Republic of the Congo or Rwanda. As for the victims, went this school of thought, they must have been Rwandan, Kenyan or Tanzanian. How else could they disappear from their homes for long periods without anybody noticing and alerting the authorities?

No-one championed this view as eloquently and enthusiastically as the ruling party boss of one of Uganda's central districts. The party apparatchik who was a master spin-doctor claimed the dead cultists were all Tutsi, from neighbouring Rwanda. In a lamentable and theatrical rhetoric during a public rally he challenged locals to raise their hands if any had lost a relative at the hands of the Kibwetere group. Since nobody put a hand up he concluded this was proof enough that the dead cultists were non-Ugandans[73] . The trouble was that some Ugandans drew solace from chasing mirages and wasting time in defending the indefensible. Kibwetere was truly Ugandan and so were most, if not all, of his victims.

The Ugandan police did not allow itself to get side-tracked by the triviality of Kibwetere's ethnicity or nationality. A crime had been committed and those responsible had to be brought to book. Subsequently an arrest warrant was issued for the three leading cult leaders. Also sought by the police were three other cult members: Father John Kamagara, the movement treasurer; Father John Mary Kasapurali, the group's public relations man, and Ursula Komuhangi, described as an assistant with the movement. And the judge investigating the case was a man in a hurry. He wanted the police to present the criminals in his courtroom by 8th May 2000. To expedite their investigations a reward of US $ 1,300 awaited anyone who could provide police with information leading to the arrest and prosecution of any of the wanted six. It was a generous reward considering that the total sum, which amounted to US $ 7,800, was far more than the police budget of Kanungu sub-district. This provoked some to question the wisdom of such a reward. Instead, these critics argued, the money would have been better spent on improving the police force so that future incidents of this nature were nipped in the bud.

The six cult leaders would be charged with multiple counts of murder and if convicted, death by hanging would follow. It was generally assumed that at least some of the key leaders had escaped the inferno and were on the run. A tough-talking Mr. Museveni, in his characteristic chivalrous style, even offered to hunt the cult leaders personally. "If it is true that … the leaders are alive, I may have to go there and join in the hunt.[74]" Uganda was determined to apprehend and bring the cult leaders to justice. Britain, United States, Germany, Italy, Kenya and South Africa were even requested to come to Uganda's aid and provide detectives to track down Kibwetere and his apostles. Portraits of the wanted cult leaders were circulated to Interpol agencies around the world. The problem was that if Kibwetere and his associates had indeed escaped to safety, nobody had the faintest idea as to their possible whereabouts[75].

A few days after the Kanungu inferno a Catholic priest claimed to have received a telephone call from Father Dominic Kataribabo. The excommunicated priest is reported to have feigned total ignorance about the fire that burned over five hundred cult followers to death. He also vigorously denied any knowledge of the mass graves; his hands were clean. Intriguingly, the Police claimed to be monitoring Father Dominic Kataribabo's telephone conversations but could not determine the exact co-ordinates of the defrocked priest's location. Was it a genuine phone call? Or was it just a ruse by someone bent on making mischief and the real Kataribabo was the man wearing a Roman collar in the ashes of the Kanungu chapel?

Some people believed that surviving cult leaders had crossed into the neighbouring Democratic People's Republic of the Congo seeking protection from their *interahamwe* friends. The Allied Democratic Front (ADF), a rebel group of Muslim fundamentalists operating from the Mountains of the Moon from where its fighters descended to the valleys to hack villagers to death, claimed to be harbouring Kibwetere. This was not a completely outrageous boast given the violent history of the two groups, some observers noted.

The ADF claimed it was willing to hand Kibwetere over to the government in exchange for certain concessions. Most likely the group wanted the government to release and hand over some of their most notorious fighters first in exchange for a man who was not in their camp. But the government would not be subjected to empty blackmail. Reports then started filtering in from western Kenya that Joseph Kibwetere might be taking refuge there.

It is instructive to note that western Kenya is an interesting place in terms of religious diversity. It could easily be home to the highest number of religious sects found anywhere in East Africa. Leaders of these sects are known for their extravagant claims. For example, Elijah Masinde, the founder of a group calling itself ***Dini Ya Musambwa*** (Religion of the Spirit) built a strong following based on outrageous claims. "I have spoken to God on several occasions. He assures me that I will be the only person to remain at the end of the world," he had preached to Kenyans. The fact, however unglamorous, that the supposedly immortal Elijah has long since died has not deterred new followers signing up for a pew in the numerous churches of the ***Religion of the Spirit***.

It is also in western Kenya that a man has shaken off all pretences at modesty and claims not to be Jesus Christ or some prophet, but that he is God himself. The man (for in spite of all his grandiose claims to being Jehovah your author still considers him to be a mortal human of flesh and blood), Jehovah Wanyonyi, claims to have unleashed AIDS on this sinful world and still has more pestilence in store for humanity. However, if the Kenyan government or the international community offered him a ransom of a few million dollars he would reconsider this threat and call off all existing pestilence. And there are many thronging to the little village, on the slopes of Mount Elgon, to see the self-styled Almighty, attended to constantly by one of his thirty or so wives. Some of his followers claim that he regularly heals the terminally ill[76].

It is also in this region that worshipping the devil, complete with human sacrifices, cannibalism and black Masses is common occurrence. Kibwetere could surely live comfortably in the area. East Africa human rights activists were so concerned about the possible presence of Kibwetere in western Kenya that they called upon the Kenyan government to take the claims seriously and conduct a thorough investigation.

Meanwhile in neighbouring countries, governments were worried that eccentric leaders of fringe religious groups might seek to imitate or even worse, outperform the Kibwetere cult. In Rwanda the authorities moved swiftly to detain eight members of an organisation calling itself ***Minevam***. ***Minevam*** had been urging followers to dedicate their waking hours to prayer. It seemed to have a number of things in common with the Kibwetere cult.

The Kenyan government also was gripped by panic. Particularly worrying were claims of mysterious killings in western Kenya thought to be the work of a satanic cult called ***Jiongo***. For some strange reason practitioners of the cult were said to require fresh human sexual organs, tongues and eyes for their worship. The ***Jiongo*** were said to launch their raids for human organs during nocturnal hours.

In Tanzania, the chairman of the ruling party youth wing suggested that a bishop of the ***Full Gospel Bible Fellowship*** might lead his followers to commit mass suicide. Naturally the bishop was not amused. Heavily aggrieved, he demanded that the chairman apologise and retract his remark within a week or else his God would show the party boss the difference between the bishop and Kibwetere. Shaken at what the bishop's God might do, the chairman promptly apologised.

Throughout the region bizarre tales began surfacing. Village folk were left feeling even more vulnerable than ever before. In this highly charged atmosphere of fear and suspicion, it was virtually difficult to separate fiction from fact[77]. Because Kanungu had happened, so went the general consensus, far more evil things were capable of happening. Parents became unusually protective of their children, not daring to leave them to play outside the watchful eyes of a trusted adult. Travel after sunset became greatly curtailed. Kanungu had affected social life.

Elsewhere in Africa, governments began talking loudly about monitoring dangerous religious groups. Belonging to religious groups that the majority perceived as meeting their definition of a cult became dangerous business. Even members of the most innocent of religious groups began getting jittery by the extra scrutiny.

In eastern Uganda a small Christian charity organisation had started an orphanage for children who had lost their parents to AIDS. A petty government official paid a visit to the director of the orphanage a few weeks after Kanungu. The official let it be known that the leaders of the orphanage were to be closely monitored henceforth. Bewildered, the orphanage director begged the official for an explanation of this atypical protocol. Well, said the official, he suspected the group was interested in collecting orphans, indoctrinating them in satanic religion and then setting them ablaze.

A cabinet minister, distantly related to some of the Kanungu cult leaders, accused those campaigning against the ruling party's "movement" system in favour of pluralism, as followers of Kibwetere. In Kampala a mob came close to lynching an unsuspecting couple seen chatting in sign language. The mob closed in on the man and woman, accusing both of being Kibwetere's followers or belonging to an even more sinister cult. "Prove that you are not cultists," the angry crowds shouted at the couple. But the two poor souls refused to answer the irate mob. Instead they gesticulated vigorously with their hands and made unintelligible noises. Just when someone in the crowd was about to stone the couple, a passer-by observed that the crowd was gearing up to lynch her deaf and dumb neighbours. Those relying on sign language to communicate were in trouble. Paranoia had arrived in Uganda.

In the first few months after Kanungu nobody provoked as much paranoia as anyone clad as a priest or nun. The nun's habit, once a symbol of virtuous living, was now associated with the charlatan Credonia Mwerinde. In the pre-Kanungu era, irrespective of their religious denomination, motorists were in the habit of offering free lifts to nuns and priests. It was something done out of a sense of deep respect to fellow humans capable of making a conscious decision to reject the enticing material things of this world and choose the often difficult path of personal deprivation that so often characterised religious life. But after Kanungu it became difficult for people to make a distinction between the impostors and truly religious and no one in their right mind risked giving a lift to those dressed as nuns or priests.

Credonia Mwerinde had dressed in a nun's habit and so did the members of the Franciscan Sisters or the Banabikira—two bona fide religious orders in Uganda. Kibwetere had gone about business clad in the vestments of a Catholic bishop and so did the bona fide bishop of any Uganda diocese. Kataribabo, although excommunicated, still wore his black shirt and white Roman collar just like his ex-colleagues in the Roman Catholic Church. The public was now suspicious of the religious. Ugandans were scrutinising their priests and nuns more closely than at any time in history. Undoubtedly the religious were uncomfortable with this new state of affairs. "The clerical collar is no longer a symbol of dignity, integrity and godliness. The fact that the leaders of the Kanungu cult wore collars has cast clerical dress and church work in sinister light," a worried director of Kampala Evangelical School of Theology lamented[78].

To make matters worse (for priests in general and the Catholic Church in particular) the embarrassing matter of another disreputable excommunicated Catholic priest was resurrected. It was alleged that Father Bishanga Kabishanga had murdered nine girls training to become nuns[79]. The gruesome incident happened on 2nd June 1978 in the remote parish of Kahunge, western Uganda, where Bishanga had served as parish priest. Found guilty by the courts, the rogue priest was sentenced to life imprisonment. But through a strange twist of events, peculiar to this part of the world, he managed to escape from prison after serving less than a year.

It is common practice in Uganda, and perhaps much of sub-Saharan Africa, that when a government is violently overthrown (sadly, the usual manner of changing governments in these parts) the jails respond by throwing their doors wide open. That is how Father Bishanga found himself a free man in 1979. Since that escape the priest had lived in relative comfort. But Kanungu had now emboldened ordinary folk to speak out and expose crimes even if they were committed by the clergy. Relatives of the victims now demanded justice.

Ironically some of the clergy on the religious right saw in the Kanungu inferno an opportunity to renew their message calling for stricter moral control in the country. A strict code of righteous living was necessary, they argued, to prevent further incidents like Kanungu. This was clearly seen a few months after Kanungu when the religious right shouted itself hoarse following a Miss Kampala beauty pageant that featured young women dressed in bikinis. These conservative clerics could not see the difference between nudity and wearing a bikini[80]. Accordingly, the fundamentalists accused the beauty contest organisers of being cultists and perpetrators of false doctrine. One pastor appealed to the government to arrest the beauty queens quickly and punish them severely. However, most mainstream clergy were content not to antagonise Christians any further by advocating moralistic values that might be interpreted as approximating the Kibwetere doctrine.

The post-Kibwetere period brought rivalries between mainstream and the so-called fringe religious groups to the fore. Mainstream clerics called on the government to move swiftly and impose a ban on cults. But nobody seemed to be clear on the criteria that a religious organisation had to meet before being labelled as a cult. One thing was certain, however. If foreigners from the East or West had introduced a religious organisation before the twentieth century then the warped Ugandan logic seemed to accept that such a group could rightly claim to belong to the religious mainstream. This meant in effect that only Catholics, Church of Uganda Protestants and Sunni Muslims were religious conformists. By definition anything falling outside this extremely novel criterion could be referred to as a cult. Hence, evangelical (born-again) Christian organisations found themselves being referred to as a cult.

In Luwero district, central Uganda, villagers were pretty happy with this definition. They demanded the closure of all born-again Christian churches and zealots torched some churches that dared remain open. Elsewhere in the country, born-again pastors were barred from preaching. And such pastors acquired the byname of "Kibwetere" overnight. Interestingly, nobody from the mainstream religious organisations showed any serious interest in restraining their followers from launching physical or verbal abuse at the born-again Christians.

This situation forced born-again Christian leaders to take the uncharacteristic step of going on the attack. They reminded Ugandans that the six leaders of the Kanungu cult wanted for the murders of their flock were originally Catholic. To further demonise the Catholic

Church a fiery Pentecostal preacher reminded Ugandans that, "The religion (Roman Catholic) which killed people in Kanungu has murdered many in the past." Allusion to the Spanish inquisition was clear in the preacher's message. The born-again camp looked at the Kanungu massacre and clearly saw the devious hand of mainstream Christian churches. According to them, mainstream churches had deliberately organised the Kanungu cult killings as a strategy to tarnish their image.

Why would the born-again church be a thorn in the side of the mainstream Christian church? Well, the born-again clergy claimed that more and more people were leaving mainstream churches and heading for the more charismatic and Holy Spirit-filled born-again churches. And the trend was set to increase, according to the born-again clergy. This was reason enough for mainstream Christian churches to turn to macabre means to address the problem of increasingly empty pews at Sunday service. Conspiracy theories had been borne.

None floated conspiracy theories with such relish as did some members of Uganda's fractured political opposition. The Kanungu killings provided the opposition with something to use in their perennial struggle to discredit the government. One opposition politician shocked the nation when he claimed that thirty-eight male bodies exhumed from under the floor of Father Kataribabo's bedroom bore characteristics not commonly encountered in that part of western Uganda. He noted that these males were circumcised, which according to him seemed to suggest they were Muslims. And just which kind of Muslim was the government interested in liquidating? Of course, the Allied Democratic Front (ADF) Muslim fundamentalist fighters captured by government troops from their Mountain of the Moon stronghold!

According to this conspiracy theory, in the immediate aftermath of Kanungu, the state discerned a golden opportunity to get rid of the intransigent Muslim rebels it was holding captive. After murdering the rebels, state agents dumped them in hurriedly dug shallow graves at numerous cult compounds in full knowledge that the cult could be blamed for these murders. Circumstantial evidence was available to support this allegation, proponents of this line of reasoning insisted.

This conspiracy theory did not doubt that the Kanungu inferno was the work of the cult but questioned if the cult should be blamed for those dumped in mass graves on cult property.

Predictably Muslim sentiments were stirred. When the ADF decided to wage guerrilla warfare as a way of bringing down Mr. Museveni's government and paving way for the establishment of strict Islamic law in Uganda, Muslims are reported to have suffered continuous harassment at the hands of state agents. A number of Muslim youths had been accused of belonging to the ranks of the rebels and were held at numerous jails throughout the country. Relatives were not given the opportunity to visit. Therefore, the claims of the opposition politician seemed to make lots of sense to the Muslim community.

During Friday prayers an Imam repeated the claims of the opposition politician and further alleged that the so-called "safe houses" run by the Internal Security Organisation (ISO), the country's much feared security and intelligence agency, might be home to mass graves. The Imam wouldn't be surprised, he said, if the cult's Kampala house with the mass grave was one of these notorious "safe houses", where people opposed to the government were routinely tortured and killed. He demanded an independent inquiry into the matter. Even Uganda's most respected opposition politician, Dr. Paul Semogerere, insisted that an international commission of inquiry be formed to probe the cult deaths since it appeared government was eager to hide something.

In its turn the government was not doing much to dispel these outlandish theories. If anything its conduct appeared to confirm the conspiracy theory. For instance, when more mass graves were discovered, the authorities were quick to bar journalists from the sites. This move seemed to confirm a cover-up of sorts on part of the government.

Another conspiracy theory claimed that the murdered victims belonged to Rwanda's Hutu ethnic group. According to this account, the Tutsi-dominated Rwanda government sought to avenge the deaths of their brethren during the 1994 genocide by killing as many Hutus as possible. After all, most of the *interahamwe* were Hutus and most of their victims were Tutsi. Somehow, the Rwandan government had hired Kibwetere and his apostles to lure the Hutus into the cult and murder them.

We have already encountered a counter conspiracy theory advanced by a ruling party functionary that those who were murdered were actually Tutsi. Furthermore, this theory claimed that Kibwetere was an *interahamwe* agent obsessed with the total elimination of the Tutsi—a process attempted in 1994. Absurd as these conspiracy theories might be, some folks found them plausible.

It is commendable that amidst all these inflammatory accusations and peddling of half-truths the state didn't panic and arrest the theorists (especially those accusing the government of a hand in the deaths), as might have been expected of an African government. Although the minister of internal affairs made some angry noises at the Imam, the matter was not pursued further[81] . This is perhaps a sign that Uganda's one party system was working when it came to exercising free speech, which is undoubtedly a prerequisite for greater democracy.

Conclusion

The depths of human gullibility are unfathomable. After a harrowing incident such as the Kanungu killings, one would think that a strong precedent had been created to deter the dangerously unstable of spirit, or the spiritually derelict from falling prey to the magical allure of spiritual charlatans. But such a presupposition conveniently ignores the fact that as long as there are people claiming a special calling, however ridiculous, there will always be others willing to follow them.

Just a month after the cult killings Sodona Kehuki Kyinkuhaire, a 62-year old first cousin of Joseph Kibwetere and former employee of the wife of a high-ranking Ugandan politician, tried to build a following on the ruins of the ***Movement for the Restoration of the Ten Commandments of God***. She set her headquarters up at Mbuye, the very place that Specioza Munkatabona claimed to have had regular apparitions with the Virgin Mary. Sodona claimed to have been visited by the Virgin Mary and Father Dominic Kataribabo. The priest promised to return from heaven and explain the greater purpose of the 17th March 2000 inferno. The two had instructed her to continue with the good work begun by her cousin, Joseph Kibwetere. "Repent before the end of the present time," Sodona exhorted villagers.

Most folk might feel inclined to dismiss these claims as nonsensical. For some people, however, this was not so. They clutched at every word that this elderly woman spoke. To them Sodona was a true prophetess. When she invited the faithful to prepare for the end of the world at her Mbuye headquarters, some seventy people, including former Kibwetere cult followers who had survived the Kanungu inferno assembled. Despite the fall from grace of Specioza Munkatabona, the teenager who took western Uganda by storm with tales of visions, Mbuye still had its allure. Followers of Sodona believe that bathing in the little stream (site of the Virgin Mary's appearance to both Specioza Munkatabona and Sodona) heals AIDS and numerous ailments that afflict the people of Africa. Many travel from afar to bathe in its waters.

And Sodona was not the only seer post-Kibwetere claiming divine revelation. Numerous other men and women continue to travel the country claiming equally intriguing apparitions and special callings. Some have claimed to chat frequently with none other than God himself. Others have said Archangel Michael or Gabriel had given them healing powers. One man, a former chicken seller, took to riding a donkey round rural Ugandan villages claiming he was the last prophet, and that God had instructed him to retrace the path Jesus rode on the way to Jerusalem. However bizarre and outrageous the claims, there are always people willing to give these men and women the benefit of the doubt and jump on the spiritual bandwagon. But again, as Kanungu showed, quite a few of these religious groups are capable of leading hundreds of vulnerable people to a brutal death.

Notes

[1] King Mwanga kept a harem of young men. For a more detailed account of the King's sexual taste and his zealous persecution of early Christians see Faupel J.F. *African holocaust: the story of the Uganda martyrs*. St. Paul publications, 1962.

[2] For a greater part of its post-colonial period a Protestant political elite has governed Uganda.

[3] By 2003 adult HIV prevalence rate in the country had fallen to 5 percent from over 20 percent in the early 1990s.

[4] The name Auma bears an interesting resemblance to the infamous Japanese Aum cult that released sarin gas on the Tokyo metro. For a more detailed account of Alice Lakwena and her rebel force, see Behrend H, *Alice Lakwena and the holy spirits: war in northern Uganda, 1985-97* (Eastern African studies). Ohio University Press, 2002.

[5] In December 2001 the Bush administration included Kony's gang of murderers and rapists on its list of terrorist groups. The story of a courageous nun who ventured into Kony's camp to rescue one hundred and thirty nine schoolgirls abducted forcibly from her school by Lord's Resistance Army rebels is narrated in Els de Temmerman's *The Aboke girls. Children abducted in northern Uganda*. Fountain Publishers, 2001.

[6] Many other youngsters are reported to have embarked on stealing as means of raising enough money to secure a comfortable place in heaven (for a detailed account see *The Monitor*, 20 September 1999).

[7] For a candid and hilarious treatment of this issue see F.D.R Gureme, Forget 'third term'; let's talk about sex, *The Monitor* (7 January 2004).

[8] Fossey's work protecting mountain gorillas is the subject of a Hollywood movie, *Gorillas in the mist*. Also see Nicholas Gordon, *Murders in the mist: who killed Dian Fossey?* Hodder & Stoughton, 1993.

[9]For a more detailed treatment on the Kibeho apparitions see *Apparitions in Kibeho, Africa*, 101 Foundation (www.101foundation.

com).

[10] Drew Mariani produced a video, *Kibeho, Africa - Mary speaks to the world*, showing ecstatic young people during an apparition.

[11] Two seers, Marie-Claire and Emmanuel, didn't survive the 1994 genocide; they were butchered by the *interahamwe*.

[12] Before the 1994 genocide French and Kinyarwanda were the official languages in Rwanda. However, following the overthrow of the Hutu political elite by largely Tutsi rebels, born and raised in Anglophone Uganda, English was introduced as an official language as well.

[13] AIDS in Uganda was first recognised in Rakai district in 1982.

[14] Specioza Munkatabona claimed to have been at Kibeho during the apparitions, and that she had had a vision of the Virgin Mary like the other seers. However, some people have claimed she had never set foot in Kibeho.

[15] On 13 May 2000 the Vatican described the nature of the vision, which speaks of a bishop clothed in white falling to the ground as if he had been shot. The vision was interpreted as referring to the 1981 assassination attempt on Pope John Paul II.

[16] Some accounts have it that Kibwetere and Credonia were lovers.

[17] See the movement's publication, A timely message from heaven: the end of the present times.

[18] In 1963 Kibwetere established his own school in Ntungamo district of Uganda.

[19] Idi Amin was obsessed with high sounding titles, which he generously awarded himself from time to time. For example he forced Makerere University to award him an honorary doctorate. He would work himself into a tizzy if not addressed by his full titles: His Excellency, The Life President of the Republic of Uganda, Al Hajji Field Marshall Dr. Idi Amin Dada, V.C (Victoria Cross), D.S.O (Distinguished Service Order), M.C (Military Cross), C.B.E (Commander of the British Empire).

[20] During Idi Amin's eight-year reign of terror an estimated 500,000 people met their death at the hands of Amin's paramilitary forces.

[21] Kabale district shares a long border with Rwanda. When Kibwetere sought refuge here the Kibeho apparitions were still ongoing.

[22] Kataribabo served as rector of St. Francis Xavier Seminary, Kitabi

(Western Uganda) in the late 1970s through to the early 1980s.
[23] A Loyola Marymount spokesman described him as an "ordinary and undistinguished" student (Sheila MacVicar, ABC News, 10 April 2000)
[24] Makerere University has variously been referred to as the "Oxford" or "Harvard" of Africa.
[25] *New Vision* journalist Mathias Mugisha interviewed Fr. Ikazire soon after the March 2000 inferno.
[26] This is a local alcohol beverage made from sweet bananas. It is also Kanungu's chief export to the rest of the country.
[27] The cult's standard work (*A timely message from heaven: the end of the present times*) has more details on Angelina Migisha's apparitions.
[28] In fact Uganda's Catholic prelate Cardinal Wamala was eager to see the rebel priest return to the church. Accordingly he instructed one of his bishops to talk some sense to Kataribabo.
[29] The school was dedicated to Mary and Jesus, and also to the memory of Paul Kashaku, Credonia's father.
[30] Credonia reportedly told Theresa that a "heavenly fire" had burnt the clothes, suggesting it was a supernatural act.
[31] *New Vision* (3 April 2000).
[32] The presidential commission reported that Nabaasa's claims were not genuine. Nonetheless this has not deterred the prophetess' followers. Writing in the government-controlled newspaper, an adherent of the group claimed that Nabaasa had "close relationships with big people *in government* (emphasis mine)... a sign that she is not a quack" (*New Vision* 28 March 2003).
[33] A number of Catholic nun congregations have discarded the traditional habit, which over the years had symbolised sisterhood.
[34] Theresa separated from her husband in 1992.
[35] It so happens that at the time of Paul Kashaku's death Credonia's mother was also sick, and Credonia wanted her dead as well. The idea was to show the faithful that God had called her parents at the same time, a message that might have gone to reinforce her mysticism.
[36] Drumming is an integral part of worship in many African Christian churches today. It is possible Kibwetere's group perceived the drum as a pagan instrument fit for performing barbaric rites, an atti-

tude that was prevalent among mainstream African Christian churches only a few decades ago.

[37] This is not unlike most "born again" Christian churches in Uganda that categorise tobacco smoking and drinking of alcoholic beverages as a grave sin. Interestingly some of these groups seem to think it is okay to consume expensive imported wines.

[38] Uganda has an alarming rate of road traffic accidents, which are the fifth highest cause of death in the country (*The Monitor* 17 July 2003).

[39] Nanyonga did not make a penny out of the soil business. She died a poor woman in May 2000 after a bout of typhoid fever.

[40] The Legion of Mary is an international movement of lay Catholics that is approved by the Church.

[41] William Kamm is the leader of a group calling itself Order of Saint Charbel, which is also known as Marian Workers of Atonement. It is estimated to have 500,000 followers.

[42] Hundreds of thousands of people were made homeless, and hundreds of others died following weeks of torrential rains that hit Mozambique in February 2000. The rains flooded an area as big as the state of New Jersey.

[43] There are several excellent books on the 1994 genocide in Rwanda, such as, Philip Gorevitch's *We wish to inform you that tomorrow we will be killed with our families. Stories from Rwanda.* Picador, 1999, and the Ugandan scholar M. Mamdani's *When victims become killers. Colonialism, nativism and the genocide in Rwanda.* Princeton University Press, 2002.

[44] Middleton J. Lugbara religion: ritual and authority among an East African people. Smithsonian Institution Press, 1987.

[45] For almost two decades, Uganda belonged to that dwindling group of African states that resisted introduction of multiparty democracy. The ruling National Resistance Movement (NRM) of President Museveni has argued that multiparty democracy is bad for the African, claiming that it only breeds ethnic and religious sectarianism. Idi Amin argued as much.

[46] UN Security Council. Report of the panel of experts on the illegal exploitation of the natural resources and other forms of wealth of the Democratic Republic of the Congo (S/2001/357) 12 April 2001. Another top-secret UN report that was presented to the UN Secu-

rity Council December 2003 also detailed the roles of Uganda and Rwanda in the systematic plundering of the Democratic Republic of the Congo.

[47] Burnt hair was supposed to keep satanic forces at bay (*The Monitor* 7 April 2000).

[48] Theresa's apparition is detailed in the cult's spiritual book, *A timely message from heaven: the end of present times.*

[49] The woman couldn't stand the humiliation and subsequently deserted the group and re-married. Her husband remained with the cult and probably perished in the March 2000 inferno. Uganda Human Rights Commission. *The Kanungu massacre. The Movement for the Restoration of the Ten Commandments of God indicted* (2002).

[50] There were reports of cannibalism in the war-torn Ituri region of the Democratic Republic of the Congo as recent as 2003. Warring militias hunted down and ate the forest dwelling pygmies in the belief that pygmy flesh conferred magical powers. Sinafasi Makelo, a representative of the pygmy community made a passionate plea to the United Nations saying, "Pygmies are being pursued in the forests. People have been eaten. This is nothing more, nothing less, than a crime against humanity." BBC News 23 May 2003. See story at http://news.bbc.co.uk/2/hi/africa/2933524.stm.

[51] Reports in the Uganda press claimed that a day or so before the inferno Kataribabo had bumped into a former classmate, a Catholic bishop. However, the bishop has since denied ever meeting Kataribabo on the said date (*New Vision* 29 March 2000).

[52] There are conflicting reports regarding Kibwetere's whereabouts on that fateful day. In fact some people claim Kibwetere had most probably died of AIDS in 1999. Uganda Human Rights Commission. *The Kanungu massacre. The Movement for the Restoration of the Ten Commandments of God indicted* (2002). However, some cultists who survived the inferno claim that he was manifestly present and supervised some of the activities that took place on 17th March 2000.

[53] The lad, Ahimbisibwe, a cult member who must have known the cult leaders rather well, claimed he had seen Kibwetere and Credonia leaving the camp, and that they were not on the premises on 17th March 2000. Ahimbisibwe survived the inferno (*New Vision* 23 March 2000).

[54] *Obushera* is a sweet porridge-like sorghum drink.
[55] In 1999 *interahamwe* rebels operating from the Democratic Republic of Congo butchered eight western tourists who were visiting Uganda's Bwindi National Park, home to the rare mountain gorillas.
[56] The Uganda Human Rights Commission was unequivocal in denouncing the manner in which prisoners were used to bury the dead cultists.
[57] Idi Amin died on 16th August 2003 at King Faisal Specialist Hospital (Saudi Arabia) from complications due to multiple organ failure. He was buried in Saudi Arabia.
[58] Since 1997 Ms Mitima, a retired nurse, had tried to get the authorities to investigate the cult. She lost eighteen relatives in the fire that engulfed the cult's compound in Kanungu.
[59] *New Vision* (29 March 2000).
[60] Both Mr. Museveni and Mr. Mugabe distinguished themselves with their anti-homosexual rhetoric. However, outside this area the two men weren't exactly friends having chosen to back rival sides in an internal conflict in the Democratic Republic of the Congo with devastating consequences to the lives of their own men and those of the citizens of the Congo.
[61] *New Vision* (28 September 1999).
[62] Uganda Human Rights Commission. The Movement for the Restoration of the Ten Commandments of God indicted (2002).
[63] This claim is made in a report the movement submitted to the non-governmental board in January 2000. *The Monitor* ran a slightly edited version of the report (see *The Monitor* 25 March 2000). However, Mr. Museveni said he had never heard of the cult until it incinerated hundreds of its followers (*New Vision* 24 March 2000).
[64] *New Vision* (2 April 2000).
[65] Since the referendum the ruling NRM government has bowed to massive domestic and international pressure and allowed opposition political parties to operate in the country.
[66] Most Ugandans have always supported Mr. Museveni in his efforts to rid the country of these guerrilla groups, which are led by groups of callous killers eager to create a state subject to total anarchy.
[67] According to some estimates the war in the Congo has claimed some 3 million people.

[68] Responding to critics of his attempts to manipulate the constitution in order to run for the presidency after expiration of his two-term limit in 2006, Mr. Museveni suggested he was equal to Jesus Christ and by extension the only Ugandan with the moral authority and right political vision to lead the nation (see *The Monitor* 28 December 2003).

[69] *The East African* (7 April 2000).

[70] Paul Kabunanuki, the director of the Independent Bible Scholars, claimed that Mathew 19:21 fully legitimised Kibwetere's ideology that required followers to sell off their property in pursuit of God's kingdom. He also cited Exodus 12:12, which he said clearly showed God killing innocent children and since Kibwetere was acting on behalf of this same God he was right to do likewise (*The Monitor* 12 April 2000).

[71] Mrs Kazibwe was appointed Uganda's vice president in 1994, making her Africa's first woman to hold such a senior political post. She held the position until her forced resignation in 2003. Officially, however, it was claimed that the 48-year old had resigned in order to pursue a doctorate at Harvard.

[72] Accusations have persisted that Kazibwe misappropriated the US $2.1 million that government had obtained from donors for construction of valley dams to ease perennial water shortage in parts of the country. When asked to explain what became of the dams that were paid for but never constructed Kazibwe retorted that those querying her were "functionally illiterate for not seeing the valley dams when they were standing on them!" Johnson Nkuuhe. *Parliamentary accountability and the international financial institutions*. The 1999 Laurentian Gordon Centre, Queens University, 18-25 July 1999.

[73]However, this ruling party official grudgingly conceded that the dead might have included some few Ugandans native to the western region since it was virtually impossible to differentiate western Uganda locals from Rwandans by merely looking at their physical features (*The Monitor* 28 June 2000).

[74] *Newsweek* (3 April 2000).

[75] In a bizarre tale a Ugandan parliamentarian claimed, without any substantiation, that Kibwetere had managed to flee to Israel where he lived incognito after undergoing plastic surgery (*New Vision* 8

May 2003). Kibwetere's wife, however, spoke of her conviction that her husband had died in the inferno. She had seen a burnt body with a golden ring on the fingers. As the self-styled bishop of the cult it was only Kibwetere that was allowed to wear a "bishop's ring".

[76] More on this charismatic character at http://news.bbc.co.uk/2/hi/world/africa/1651884.stm

[77] An April Fools' Day prank that possibly originated in one of Nairobi's slums had it that Kibwetere and other cult leaders had been apprehended, and were being held for questioning at a Nairobi police station. What followed was a truly comical flurry of activities as the world's international press out-performed each other, running from one police station to another in search of the fugitives. Some international newspapers, having missed out on the humorous side so evident in Africa's slums, even ran colourful stories of the capture of the elusive cult leaders.

[78] *The East African* (24 April 2000).

[79] *The Monitor* (10 April 2000).

[80] Throughout history Ugandan males have had trouble relating with scantly clad women be they in bikinis or otherwise. In the early 1970s Idi Amin, Uganda's ex-military dictator, banned the popular miniskirt. More recently many politicians have accused dancing troupes featuring scantly dressed women of peddling immorality. The rabid rhetoric of some politicians against what is perceived as lax and shameless western moral standards is of a nature that one might associate with a theocracy. A well-publicised case in point was the arrest and harassment of Amanda's Angels, a popular group of young female artists who used to perform dances in Kampala clubs (*The Monitor* 24 April 2003). There is also an ongoing effort to ban popular striptease shows claiming that they promote immorality and the spread of AIDS. Interestingly, most of these self-styled guardians of morality are known to have numerous concubines and would probably resist any attempts to ban extra-marital sex, a major risk factor in the spread of AIDS.

[81] *New Vision* (5 May 2000).

Write for our free catalog of other fascinating books, videos & magazines

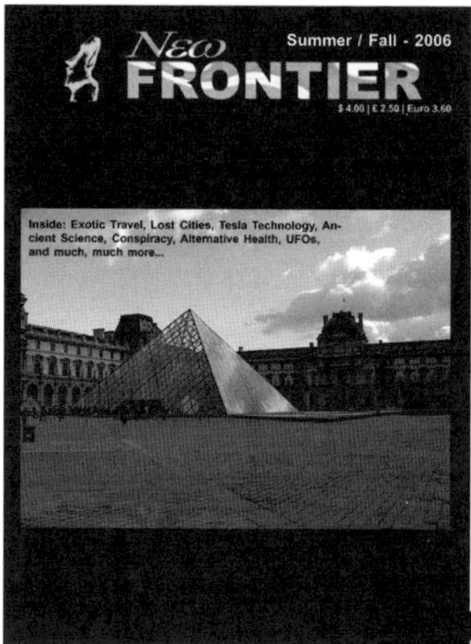

Frontier Sciences
Foundation
Postbus 10681
1001 ER Amsterdam
tel: 020-3309151
fax: 020-3309150
email : info@fsf.nl

website : www.fsf.nl

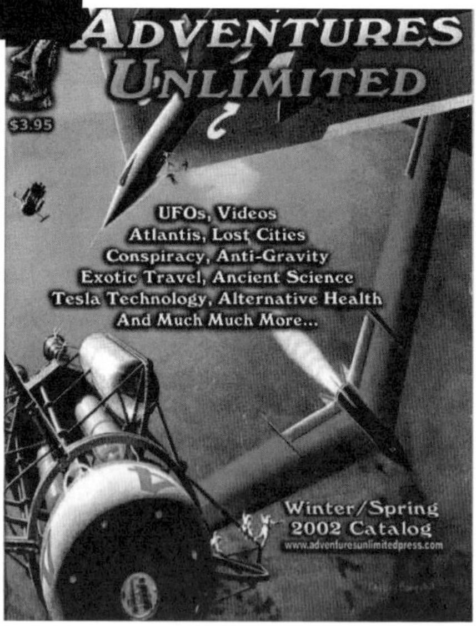

Adventures Unlimited
P.O. Box 74
Kempton
Illinois 60946
USA
Tel : 815-253-6390
Fax : 815-253-6300
email :
auphq@frontiernet.net

website : www.adventuresunlimitedpress.com